# SETH
### A·N·D
# SAMONA

# SETH

## A·N·D

# SAMONA

## JOANNE HYPPOLITE

♦

### ILLUSTRATED BY COLIN BOOTMAN

DELACORTE PRESS

Published by
Delacorte Press
Bantam Doubleday Dell Publishing Group, Inc.
1540 Broadway
New York, New York 10036

**Library of Congress Cataloging-in-Publication Data**

Hyppolite, Joanne.
Seth and Samona / Joanne Hyppolite;
illustrated by Colin Bootman.
p.    cm.
Summary: A Haitian American boy and an African American girl deal
with the fun and problems of friendship and family life.
ISBN 0-385-32093-0
1. Haitian Americans—Juvenile fiction.   [1. Haitian
Americans—Fiction.   2. Friendship—Fiction.
3. Family life—Fiction.]
I. Bootman, Colin, ill.   II. Title.
PZ7.H9897Se   1995
[Fic]—dc20                                   94-36719      CIP      AC

The text of this book is set in Berkeley Book.
Book design by Susan Clark
Manufactured in the United States of America
May 1995
10 9 8 7 6 5 4 3 2 1

In memory of *grannè-mwen,*
Amelie "Manchoune" Stinville (1904–1993),
and for my parents, Claude and Gisele.

Who could have asked for more?

# CHAPTER

## 1

I remember the first thing I thought, the day I met Samona Gemini. She was standing behind Mrs. Gray, our third-grade teacher, with her short hair cornrowed tight to her scalp and making one horrible face after another while Mrs. Gray introduced her to the class. That wasn't the worst part either. Right there in front of the entire third-grade class of Atticus Elementary, she was wearing a pair of underpants so red that you could see them through her white skirt. Everybody was giggling but all I could do was stare with shock. Right then and there I thought, "That Samona Gemini is one crazy girl and I plan to stay away from her." I remember it so well 'cause I've been saying the same thing for two years now, and though I try to stay away from girls as much as possible, that particular one has managed to make me her accomplice in trouble time and time again. Like last summer when she talked me into helping sell this all-natural homemade shampoo door-to-door 'cause it was gonna make us a million bucks but she forgot to tell everyone, including me, that the special ingredient in it was horse manure. The few people who used it were stinking for days after, and me and Samona had to hide out before they stopped looking for us. Or the time our class went on a field trip to the zoo and she said she knew a shortcut to the concession stands and landed us right in the middle of Monkey Paradise with the chimpanzees. We weren't allowed to go on field trips for the rest of the year.

It doesn't help that everybody thinks Samona's my special responsibility. Right after Samona's family moved to Boston, her mother saw my mother in the supermarket and it turned out that they'd known each other from way back in New York City when my mother first came to the United States. Manmi made it my special assignment to get to know Samona and make her feel like she belongs here. I did it 'cause I had to and 'cause when you get down to it, I'm a nice person, but ever since then I haven't been able to get rid of Samona.

After two years, you would think I would know how to avoid her, but she has a knack for tracking me down. Take last Wednesday afternoon when she came running down my street, shouting my name at the top of her lungs in broad daylight and looking a pitiful sight. Her hair was in braids to keep it from sticking out all over the place, 'cause she'd tried to hot-comb it herself the other day and made a mess of it. My first instinct was to hide but as it happened there wasn't a single parked car or thick green hedge in sight. I stuck myself behind one of those straggly baby trees they plant in the middle of gray city blocks to try and make them look better.

Despite the fact that I'm about as skinny and dark as that tree, she picked me right out. Then from all the way across the street that I have to live on, she put her hands on her hips and shouted, "Are you going to the bathroom behind that tree, Seth Michelin? 'Cause I know you were raised better than that, and anyway you're in civilization now!"

While I just about died of embarrassment, she waved to all the people who'd stuck their heads out of their windows and were looking down at us. I knew by tomorrow word would be all over the neighborhood that I had tried to pee outside on the sidewalk.

"What do you want, Samona?" I asked when my face stopped burning. The worst thing you could do was ignore Samona when she had her mind set on conversing with you.

"I want you to come over with me to Mrs. Fabiyi's." Samona smiled cheerfully like she hadn't just said the stupidest thing in the whole world.

"Mrs. Fabiyi? That batty old Nigerian lady? How can you go over there when she threw that pot of cold vegetable soup at us on Halloween?"

"I think it was potato soup, and anyway I don't think she's there or maybe something's wrong with her. She hasn't shouted out the window at me in a week. We

3

can bring her some food or something in case she's sick. Want a piece of gum?" She held out a squashed piece of Juicy Fruit.

I took it and stuck it in my mouth. "Well, that's a beautiful sentiment, Samona Gemini, but what do you really want to go over there for?"

Samona snapped her gum and shifted her weight so that her hip stuck out at an angle. As usual, she was wearing clothes that didn't fit. The shirt that she had on had to be her brother Nigel's. I learned quick never to say anything about her clothes to Samona. She'd only ask me whether I preferred that she should run around buck naked. I can't keep a straight face after she says that.

"Weeelll, Nightmare ran over there last night and she hasn't come back yet. I want you to help me find her."

Nightmare was Samona's black cat.

"That cat has scratched me every time I go over to your house. Besides, you know she'll come back when she feels like it. Why should I help you find her?"

" 'Cause then you'll get to see what Mrs. Fabiyi's house looks like. Everybody's always talking about the creepy things she keeps in there. Now we can see if it's for real or not." Samona leaned forward like she was getting to the best part. "We'll be the coolest kids in the fifth grade if we do it."

"I'd rather be alive than cool." I tried to sound grumpy but the truth was I had a piano lesson that afternoon and even going over to Mrs. Fabiyi's was better than that. "But I guess I can't let you go alone."

"You're not doing me any favors, Seth Michelin. You can tag along if you want to. Got any food we can bring to her?" Samona led the way down the street to the building I lived in. "Mama spent the grocery money on the lottery last night. Did I tell you my sister Leticia found out that Tyrone was cheating on her? She invited him over and made him an Alpo meat loaf since he was acting like such a dog. . . ."

I followed her, half-listening, half-muttering to myself. Here I'd gone and gotten myself involved with Samona again.

"Are you listening to me? It's pretty rude to go off wandering in your mind and leave a person addressing nothing but your body." Samona shook her head at me, then flounced into my apartment building like she owned the place. But once we got inside, she shut up and stood still while we went up the elevator to the fifth floor.

The strangest thing comes over Samona when she gets around my family. For one thing, she's a lot quieter. She just stands around looking and looking like we're something she's never seen before in her life. She thinks we're funny 'cause we kiss each other on the cheek all the time instead of saying hello and we pray in French before we eat and we say Manmi and Papi instead of Mom and Dad and Tant and Monnonk in-

5

stead of Aunt and Uncle. But I've been to her house enough to realize that her family are the weird ones. They're all vegetarians and eat stuff like tofu and soy milk. Samona's mother is a poet and she walks around in braids and black boots all the time talking in rhymes. When she's not being a poet, she gets dressed up in different disguises because she does undercover stories for a news magazine. The first time I met Mrs. Gemini she was dressed up like a clown because she was going undercover at a circus. And Samona's sister Leticia runs her own psychic hot line. I don't know anything about Samona's father except that he played the drums and he and Mrs. Gemini never got married. Samona doesn't like to talk about him. It was Manmi who told me that her father left them right before they moved to Boston.

Anyway, my family does all that stuff 'cause we're Haitian. Samona's family just acts weird 'cause they want to. But Samona acts so different around my family, they think she's the greatest thing since fried plantains. They think just 'cause Samona's so smart and gets straight A's that she'll rub off on me or something. Manmi is always talking about how much "life" Samona has and that I should play with her more. Like I'm a zombie or something. One time, I came home soaking wet and singing 'cause I'd pulverized Samona in a snowball fight, and the whole family went into shock. My sister Chantal kept asking me if I was okay and Granmè kept feeling my forehead. Like I don't know how to have fun or something. They never believe she's the reason for all the trouble I get into.

My granmè was the only one at home. When she saw Samona, she smiled and opened her arms to hug her, mumbling things in her low scratchy voice.

"What did she say?" Samona whispered over Granmè's shoulder.

Samona didn't understand a word Granmè said on account of the fact that Granmè only speaks Kreyol. Granmè was born in Haiti, which is on an island in the Caribbean. She came here to take care of us after her sister, Matant Margaret, and her daughter, my manmi, were already living here. Though she's lived here for a long time, Granmè still won't speak English. I was having a hard time trying to understand what she was saying myself, but for a whole different reason— Granmè had forgotten to put her teeth in again.

When she got a good look at Samona's electric hairdo, a pained expression came over her face and she murmured something else.

"She wants to know why your ma let you out of the house with your hair like that," I translated loosely before going into the kitchen.

"Don't worry, Granmè. It'll lay flat again in a couple of days," Samona said, smiling at her.

When I got into the kitchen I noticed that my sister Chantal hadn't cleaned the kitchen and washed the dishes like she was supposed to. She was probably out with her new boyfriend, Jerome. She's keeping him secret from Manmi and Papi. They would never let her have a boyfriend 'cause she's only fifteen. Chantal was going to be in big trouble if the kitchen wasn't clean before Manmi got home.

I found some fried chicken in the refrigerator and wrapped it in tinfoil. I know you're supposed to give sick people some soup but I didn't want to give Mrs. Fabiyi any ideas, since she liked throwing soup at people. Besides, I had my doubts about Mrs. Fabiyi accepting food from us, so at least Samona and I would have a good snack. I wrapped up some cookies too just in case Mrs. Fabiyi was starving.

When I came out of the kitchen I found Granmè and Samona dancing away to an old record of Tabou Combo. They're a Haitian music group that Papi likes. Samona stopped dead when she saw me, and giggled. Granmè's flowered scarf was wrapped around her head.

"Did you get some food?" Samona asked.

"Yup." I held up the bag. "Are you gonna wear that scarf outside?"

Samona scowled. "What's wrong with it?"

"Nothing," I said, but I was thinking, If you're somebody's grandmother.

"Bye, Granmè." I kissed her on the cheek and headed out the door before she could remember that I was supposed to be at my piano lesson.

As soon as Samona and I stepped out into the hall,

she took off the scarf and tied it around her leg. "I didn't want to hurt her feelings."

I nodded and we got on the elevator. I never felt quite as comfortable with Samona unless she was being her usual crazy self. By the time we were outside again, she was snapping her gum loudly and jabbering off about something or other. She didn't seem a bit worried that we might just be heading straight for trouble if Mrs. Fabiyi really was a witch.

# CHAPTER

## 2

We started out for Mrs. Fabiyi's house right away. She lives in one of those three-story houses two blocks down from our apartment. Samona lives in between on Morton Street, which is too close as far as I'm concerned.

We knew Mrs. Fabiyi's house right away 'cause it's in such bad shape. All the gray paint has just about peeled off on one side and the lawn has got so many years' worth of leaves on it that you can't see the grass. In front of the house is a big tree stump where I remember there used to be a big maple tree. Just looking at the house made me feel sad. It's like nobody cared about it.

After we stared at the house for a while, Samona looked at me and asked, "Do you think Mrs. Fabiyi ate Nightmare?"

"What the heck for?"

"Maybe she's hungry. I'd eat a cat if I were hungry enough. It's supposed to taste like chicken."

"That's 'cause you're crazy, Samona Gemini. Besides,

as evil as Nightmare is, she'd give Mrs. Fabiyi stomach problems for the rest of her life and Mrs. Fabiyi can't be all that hungry if she's throwing vegetable soup at people." I half-expected something to come flying out the window any minute.

"Well, the only way we're going to find out is to go in." Samona marched up the stairs like a general. "Are you coming or not?"

I followed her more slowly. What if Mrs. Fabiyi thought we were burglars and came after us with a baseball bat? Everybody knows she doesn't like kids.

Samona was reading the mailboxes when I caught up to her. "She lives on the third floor," she said.

"We already know that." I was beginning to get the idea that Samona wasn't as brave as she let on, but she was too proud to show it.

She put her hand on the doorknob and opened it slowly. Inside, I could just make out a dark stairwell and a dusty, narrow hallway. I thought I could hear mice scurrying around. That piano lesson was beginning to look mighty appealing.

"Maybe we should look for Nightmare outside," I suggested. It seemed like a good idea to me. Somehow I knew Samona wasn't going to go for it.

She put on one of those patient smiles teachers and doctors use to explain things to little kids. "Then we don't get to see her house. You scared of the dark or something?"

"Me? Scared?" I walked into the hallway with a stiff

back and a stomach that felt like it had lead marbles in it.

Samona closed the door behind us and we started up the stairs. It was so dark I could barely see where I was headed. I felt sticky cobwebs brush against my face. When we reached the last flight of stairs, the steps began to creak. Each step had a different kind of creak to it and each one was louder than the one before. So much for burglars. These steps were loud enough to wake the dearly departed. I was glad to see the third floor was lit by a tiny lightbulb.

Samona, however, had a spooked expression on her face as she looked around. "There's no door."

True enough, there wasn't anything but walls around us.

"Guess we'll have to go," I said cheerfully.

Samona grabbed the back of my shirt as I started down the stairs. "I didn't come all the way up here for nothing. There must be a way to get into her apartment. We have to save Nightmare."

Samona put her hands on her hips like she was trying to think of something, then walked over to one of the walls and began banging hard and loud on it.

Just as I was about to stop her from getting us both in more trouble, I saw the wall behind Samona opening up from nowhere and Samona falling down at the feet of an old lady dressed in nothing but a sheet and a scarf wrapped around her head. She also had the meanest look on her face.

"Ah-ah! You!"

Samona's eyes bugged out of her head from where she was lying on the floor as Mrs. Fabiyi began talking fast and loud and pointing and screaming. The marbles in my stomach had turned to bricks and all I could do was stand there and stare. I couldn't make out a word Mrs. Fabiyi was saying 'cause she was screaming in some other language but I could see the long stick she was waving in the air over Samona's head. Either she was going to hit us or put a spell on us.

"We came to bring you some food," I whispered finally, holding up the bag of food. "For your sickness."

"Sick?" The way Mrs. Fabiyi said it made it sound like "seek," but at least she was speaking English now. "What for?"

"So you don't have to eat cats," I blurted out before I stopped to think.

"Cat! You is sick one, boy." Mrs. Fabiyi shook her stick again. "Go!"

Samona stood up, rubbing her sore bottom. "We're not leaving until I get my cat back!"

Mrs. Fabiyi looked at her closely, then started cackling. I could see her red gums clear as could be. She must have forgotten to put her teeth in. Just like Granmè. And she had finally stopped waving that stick. Suddenly I wasn't so scared anymore.

"I know you?" Mrs. Fabiyi asked in a low whisper after she had finished laughing.

"You threw vegetable soup at us on Halloween," I reminded her.

Mrs. Fabiyi started cackling again. "Ah-ah! I remember! So much fun. Trick or treat, you! Nobody else come that night."

"I wonder why," Samona muttered. "You got my leaves all wet."

Samona had dressed up like a tree for Halloween, with real leaves pasted to her head. It took her mama two hours to wash the glue out of her hair. Then Mrs. Gemini wrote a poem about it.

"Trick or treat make you mad?" Mrs. Fabiyi looked a little upset. "I was—how you say—making fun."

"Where's my cat?" Samona put her hands on her hips.

Mrs. Fabiyi chuckled. "Big, black cat? He play with my Egusi. You come in. You are welcome."

Samona followed her through the door in the wall while I looked around a little more. The opening *was* a door. It was painted black like the rest of the wall, which seemed like a strange color to me, and it didn't have a doorknob on the outside. This was a pretty weird house.

I had to go through one of those slimy, slippery bead curtains, that was just hanging right inside the doorway. Then there was a small hallway leading to another room. I followed it, holding in my breath and saying a quick prayer. Who knew when I was gonna come back out—or if I was. What I saw there made me wish I hadn't wasted my breath. There weren't any bats in the corners or animal skeletons pinned to the walls or anything a witch is supposed to have in her house. All that was there were some normal-looking wicker chairs and some wood carvings on the wall. One of the carvings looked like the African masks our art teacher had showed us in a slide show last week. They were the only interesting things in the room.

I followed Samona's voice to the back porch, where she was petting a small tabby cat—Egusi, I guessed. Mrs. Fabiyi turned to me and made another one of those gummy smiles. In the daylight I could see that she wasn't wearing a sheet at all. It was a long blue and green and black dress that touched the floor. The scarf was made of the same material. Mrs. Fabiyi looked younger than Granmè. She had black skin that was smooth and didn't have a wrinkle in it. "Well, you. What you see?"

"There aren't any toad's eyes or voodoo dolls or even a stupid love potion." Here I'd come all this way and Mrs. Fabiyi turned out to be nothing but a regular old lady. Manmi was gonna kill me when she found out I skipped another piano lesson.

Mrs. Fabiyi's eyes twinkled. "You think I obeah-witch woman? Ah-ah! More fun to scare little boys like you."

"I wasn't scared," I said, turning away.

"Mrs. Fabiyi hasn't been sick," Samona said, cuddling the little cat. "She went to see her sister in Nigeria."

"It good for you to come see about me. You come again. I promise no more soup."

Samona put Egusi on the floor and picked up Nightmare. "That's very civilized of you, Mrs. Fabiyi. And I guess I don't mind if Nightmare comes over here to visit Egusi either."

Well, I was tired of this. No one was going to eat or kill us here. I hadn't even seen a kitchen knife around. Papi was right: You can't believe everything that people say. It's just like some of the kids at school who think that all Haitians are boat people and only eat frogs' legs. I should have known better than to believe the stories about Mrs. Fabiyi. People like to think all kinds of bad things about you just 'cause you come from someplace different.

"It was nice meeting you, Mrs. Fabiyi. I'm leaving, Samona. You can come if you want to." I headed for the front door.

Samona stuck her tongue out at my back. "You can throw soup at him anytime, Mrs. Fabiyi. Seth Michelin! Wait up!"

"You are welcome," Mrs. Fabiyi called after us. "And you right, Samona. Cat taste good as chicken."

Samona looked back at her with wide eyes before chasing me down the stairs. "See! I told you!"

I didn't pay her any mind. I started walking as fast as

I could once we got outside. The bright sunlight hit me in the eyes and made me squint.

Samona caught up with me, huffing a little and squeezing the life out of Nightmare. "What are you walking so fast for?"

I stopped. "Look, Samona. I don't have any time to be wasting with you."

She shifted Nightmare to her other arm. "Well, 'scuse me. Where's the fire?"

I glared at her. "I got places to go, okay?"

"I got places of my own to get to," Samona sniffed.

"Like what?" I asked as scornfully as possible.

"Well . . ." Samona bit her lip. "Matter of fact I have to go to the city hall today and register for the Little Miss Dorchester contest."

My mouth fell wide open. "You're off your rocker. You can't win that contest."

"Oh yeah? Wait and see." Samona pointed to my open mouth, then turned and walked away. "Better watch out for them flies."

# CHAPTER

## 3

Samona's fool idea about entering the beauty contest went right out of my head later when I opened the door to our apartment. I had my nose all wrinkled up 'cause they had just mopped the hallway and it smelled like ammonia. I knew it would stink like that for days. Sometimes Manmi smelled like that when she came home from work at the hospital. When she smells like that, it means she got stuck washing the floors all day and she usually has to go straight to bed 'cause her back hurts so much. I was wishing for the hundredth time that we could live in a real house like my cousin Enrie when I walked through the door and knew something was wrong.

For one thing, it was so dark I could barely see in front of me. All the shades had been drawn to shut out the sunlight. If it wasn't for the tiny lamp lit up in the corner of the living room, I would not have been able to make out Tant Cherise, Tant Renee and Monnonk Roddie setting up a low murmur in Kreyol on the couch. There wasn't any sign of Granmè or Manmi, and that started to make me nervous.

Then I smelled the spirits in the air and I knew Tant Renee must be drinking. I looked closer and sure enough, she was sitting in the pocket corner of the couch with her hair hanging down straggly-like and a large glass of clarin in her hand. Her face was starting to swell up like it always does when she takes to the spirits. Now, Tant Renee is a terrible drinker but she knows better than to be doing it in Manmi's home. I knew something serious must have happened.

Tant Cherise noticed me first and ran over to give me a hug so tight I could feel the bones sticking out of her body. Tant Cherise is almost as skinny as me, which is where I get it from, I guess. She's a *grimelle,* though, like Manmi and Chantal—which means she's really light-skinned. Jean-Claude and I are as dark as tree bark—like Papi.

"What's going on?" I kissed her on the cheek, automatically.

Tant Cherise put her hand over my head and all of a sudden commenced to crying and moaning at the same time in her heavy accent, *"Priye avek mwen,* Seth. Pray with me."

Her words didn't scare me as much as her crying did. Tant Cherise is about as holy as can be. She's always praying for people's souls and rejoicing over who just joined the church. But I'd never seen her carry on like this before.

Monnonk Roddie came and pulled her away from me. I could hear him whisper to her that I was just a kid, and that got me mad. I wanted to know what was going on here.

I looked up fiercely at Monnonk Roddie's coal black face and all the anger just fell away. I don't think I've ever seen Monnonk Roddie when he wasn't laughing at something. He's bald and fat and smokes too much but he's got one of those faces that is full of laughing. If it's not in his smile then it's in the corner of his eyes or the twitching of his mustache or the shaking of his furry eyebrows.

My throat was starting to feel tight. Something must be terribly wrong, with Tant Renee drinking and Tant Cherise crying and Monnonk Roddie not laughing.

"Monnonk Roddie," I finally choked out, "where's Manmi?"

Monnonk Roddie put a hand on my shoulder. "We didn't mean to scare you, Seth. Your manmi is fine. She's in there with your granmè. Granmè didn't take the news too well, and your manmi is trying to calm her down.

"What news?" I asked, feeling a little bit better. "Is Papi okay? Where's Jean-Claude and Chantal?"

"Papi's out taking care of everything for the wake and the funeral. Your granmè's sister, Margaret, died this morning—at last." Monnonk Roddie shook his head carefully, like he was afraid it would break. "Only person that ever laughed at my jokes. She was a crazy one."

Matant Margaret! Relief rushed through me. I hardly even knew her. She was ninety-four and lived in a rest home near Mattapan Square. Granmè went to visit her every Sunday and Tant Renee saw her every day but the rest of the family only saw her on Christmas. Every year we went over to the rest home to have dinner with her and the other sick old ladies. She never recognized us. All she could do was sit in her chair and stare at us with her mouth hanging open and her eyes half-closed.

Matant Margaret was dead and I wasn't sure what to feel. I knew Granmè and Manmi would be pretty sad. They were always telling stories about how Matant Margaret worked in the casinos in Haiti to save money to buy her visa and her plane ticket to America.

"Is Granmè gonna be okay?" I asked anxiously. Now I could make out the soft sound of Manmi's voice coming from Granmè and Chantal's bedroom.

Monnonk Roddie nodded. "She's just feeling a little of the pain right now, Seth. I guess we all are. You go sit with your brother and sister in your room."

I got out of there quick 'cause I knew Monnonk Roddie was gonna try to get Tant Renee to quit drinking and there was going to be a screaming fight before Tant Renee let go of that bottle.

My room wasn't as dark as the living room. The shade was pulled halfway but there was an even layer of sunlight coming from the bottom of the window. The television was sitting next to Jean-Claude's bed instead of in the living room.

My sister Chantal was sitting on one side of Jean-Claude's bed painting her toenails and running her mouth off on the phone about Jerome, who is all she talks about since they started going together.

I don't know exactly what to make of Jerome. The first time he came over to the house he had to wait for Chantal to finish washing the tub, so he started asking me all sorts of funny questions. Do I ever clean the tub? Does Chantal get good grades? Does she do all the housework? Does she get to stay out late like Jean-Claude? What does she want to be when she grows up? Does she cook all the food? I couldn't answer half the questions. I told him that Manmi and Granmè cook and do housework too. Jean-Claude and I have to keep our rooms clean. I wasn't sure but I think Chantal wants to be a nurse like Manmi.

Jerome didn't seem to like any of my answers. He didn't ask me any more questions but I heard him whisper "typical Caribbean" and something about sexism under his breath and I started to get mad. What was he talking about? Who was he to criticize my family? Chantal told me that Jerome didn't even have a big family. It was just him and his mother. I couldn't see what he was criticizing anyway since he didn't know anything about us.

Samona met Jerome once and thought that he was a lot like Jean-Claude but I didn't pay much attention to the opinion of someone who would sell shampoo made of horse manure. She talked to Jerome for a long time one day when he was waiting for Chantal on our steps.

"He seems okay to me," Samona told me after I got tired of waiting for her to go away and came outside.

I looked at her like she was crazy and then at Jerome, who was walking down the street with Chantal. Jerome was built like a football player—not very tall but with big muscles. He kept his hair really short, so he looked almost bald. But his eyes were what bothered me. They were light brown and always seemed to be looking at everything like he was trying to take it apart and understand it. It gave me the creeps.

Samona twirled one of the wooden beads in her hair. "He had to take care of his mother and his two older sisters all by himself. He thinks women should be liberated and take care of themselves."

"Liberated from what? Anyway, that's not what Jean-Claude thinks," I said. I was wondering if Samona knew that she had two completely different sandals on today. One red. One purple.

"That's 'cause Jean-Claude's just like you and all men," Samona announced. "You like to pass judgment on people and control things—at least that's what Leticia said about Tyrone."

I gave Samona a look that said she wasn't making sense as usual.

Now, back in the room, my brother Jean-Claude was lying flat beside Chantal. His long feet were sticking off the end of the bed 'cause he's so tall for seventeen. He was half-watching the news and half-listening to Chantal. Jean-Claude is always telling Chantal that Jerome is nothing but a lost brother with no kind of future. He knows Jerome quit school last year and works full-time at the 7-Eleven near the highway.

"Hi, Seth." Chantal looked up from her toenails and smiled that smile that looked just like Manmi's. Sometimes it surprises me how much Chantal can look like Manmi, with her golden skin and long, thick hair. "Is Papi home?"

"No," I said, and sat down at the edge of the bed. "You think Granmè's gonna be all right?"

"Yeah." Chantal reached out and touched my shoulder gently. "That old woman'll live forever just so I never get my own room."

I smiled at that 'cause Chantal's been asking for her own room for years. She's all the time complaining about Granmè snoring like a horse and making her do the rosary with her every night. Chantal always falls asleep before Granmè can finish.

Jean-Claude turned his attention from the news and

I was glad to see that he didn't look upset. He goes off when he hears news like something about two brothers shooting each other over a basketball game. He's always talking about how the television only shows bad images of black men on the news. They don't show the good things that black men do every day like take care of their families, or come up with all those inventions like the traffic light.

His face was still serious as he looked at us. There was a big dent in his hair and I could tell he'd been sleeping on one side of his head for a while.

"Y'all know we're gonna have to go to the wake tomorrow," he said.

"What's a wake?" I asked. Monnonk Roddie had said that Papi was out taking care of it.

Chantal's face fell. "Aww, man. I'm supposed to go out with Jerome tomorrow. Maybe he can sit in the back where Manmi and Papi wouldn't see him."

Jean-Claude turned his face back to the television and said, "Don't you dare bring that sorry brother near the wake."

"You don't even know Jerome!" Chantal almost tipped the nail polish on the bed as she sat up.

I got up off the bed and left the room. I hate it when Jean-Claude and Chantal fight. They never used to argue until Chantal started seeing Jerome. Jean-Claude must have a good reason not to like Jerome. They call Jean-Claude "the savior" out on the streets 'cause he's always the one to step in and stop a fight or if he hears about something going down, he'll go and try to talk people out of making trouble. Everybody trusts Jean-Claude.

I tiptoed down the hallway past the living room to Granmè's room. I almost tripped on the vinyl that protects the carpet from dirt but nobody saw me. The door to Granmè's room was cracked open and I peeked inside.

Granmè was lying in bed asleep. One of her hands was under her head, trapping her rosary beads against her cheek and the pillow.

She looks okay, I told myself, and then I looked up at Manmi, who was sitting on the rocking chair beside the bed. She still had on her white hospital uniform and her eyes were closed like she was asleep too. I wondered if Matant Margaret's death had made her forget about her new hairstyle. It was cut short and fell around her face. It used to be very long, longer than Chantal's. It was Samona's mother who told Manmi that her hair was too old-fashioned and that she should get something more contemporary. I told Mrs. Gemini that Haitians *like* to be old-fashioned. When Jean-Claude had gotten his hair cut into a fade, like the other guys at school, all the family and all our relatives talked about it for weeks before they got used to it. That's what Manmi was going through now. In spite of all the talk, though, I could tell Manmi liked her new haircut.

"Seth."

I jumped 'cause Manmi hadn't even opened her eyes, but somehow she'd known that I was there. Manmi can be spooky like that. She can always tell when one of us is lying, which makes it pretty hard to get away with anything.

I edged inside the room and went to kiss Manmi on the cheek. I was glad she smelled like her flowery perfume and not like ammonia. I turned back to look at Granmè again. Coming home and seeing everybody in the living room like that had really scared me.

*"Dou-dou?"* Manmi said, using her own special nickname for me. I guess she wanted to know what I was doing here, but I didn't say anything.

"Granmè is fine," Manmi said quietly. She took my hand and shook it gently like she always does when she wants me to loosen up.

"Then why's she in bed?" I asked, leaning back against her knees.

"It's always a shock, you know, when you first hear." Manmi's voice had a soft Kreyol accent. It was so subtle most people didn't notice it. "Such a serious boy God gave me. Everything is good here. Go back to your room."

I looked at Manmi and her eyes started to close again. I could tell she was really sad but she didn't want to show it in front of me. "Okay."

When I got into the hallway, I heard a loud, *"Assez! Bay tèt mwe lapé!"* which basically meant "cut it out now!" and I knew that Papi had come home and was mad with Jean-Claude and Chantal for arguing. I hurried back into the room.

Jean-Claude and Chantal were quiet. When Papi speaks to us in Kreyol, he means business. He stepped into the room, bending his head so as not to hit the doorframe. Papi was so tall I always had to bend my head way back just to look him in the eye.

"You have to be quieter so Granmè can get some sleep," Papi sighed, switching to English. He looked tired too and he changed into his blue uniform for work at the airport. Papi works on the ground crew for Air France. He likes his job 'cause he can be close to all the airplanes and learn more about them. Before he married Manmi, he wanted to be a pilot but he couldn't join the air force 'cause he wasn't a U.S. citizen and flying lessons were too expensive. I think he still dreams about being a pilot someday 'cause he drags us to every flying exhibition that comes into town. Once he took a trip on the train to Washington, D.C., all by himself to go to the Museum of Flying. He spent the whole day there and when he got back home he talked about everything he saw until he drove us crazy.

"Now, you've all heard about Matant Margaret." Papi looked at us with steady brown eyes. "Is there anything you want to talk about or ask me?"

"How's Granmè?" Chantal asked first.

"So-so." Papi smiled a little and moved a hand up to scratch his chin. "She'll be cooking your favorite *pen patat* by next week. She knew this was coming."

"When's the funeral?" Jean-Claude asked softly.

"In two days. You miss school on Friday and—"

"What about tomorrow?" I interrupted, shocked. I had been looking forward to not seeing Samona tomorrow. "Shouldn't we stay home and wear black or something?"

"No. School tomorrow like normal. Your manmi's taking the day off from work." He stopped at the sound of rising voices from the living room. It sounded like Tant Renee and Monnonk Roddie were about to get into it.

"Jean-Claude, go give your uncle some help. And you two put your shoes on. We're going out to eat so your manmi can have some rest."

Chantal and I looked at each other in surprise after Jean-Claude and Papi left the room. We hardly ever get out to eat—not even to McDonald's. Manmi can't stand for us to eat junk food. Soon my mind was so full of the thought of french fries and apple pie that it wasn't until late that night that I realized I still didn't know what this wake thing was that we were going to.

# CHAPTER

# 4

I t was Samona who finally let me in on what a wake was. All the way to school the next day my cousin Enrie and I had been talking about it and getting nowhere. Enrie was a grade lower than me and he knew even less than I did. We were just about to give up on the whole thing when I was nearly blinded for life by the sight of Samona coming into the schoolyard in one of those bright neon green sweat suits with matching socks. Just looking at her gave me a headache.

"Something wrong?" Samona asked, standing about five feet away from us with a funny look on her face. It was probably giving her shocks that I wasn't running in the other direction. But I decided right then and there that Samona might be the best person to ask about this wake thing. She was always telling me all sorts of strange things that I never even heard of and most of the time didn't want to hear about. Now maybe I could get some information out of her.

"Come here, Samona." I put on my friendliest smile and waved her over.

Samona lifted one of her black eyebrows and stood her ground. "What for?"

"I want to ask you a question," I said.

Samona moved forward slowly. The normal tone of my voice must have put her at ease. Enrie's eyes widened as he took in the way she was dressed but he didn't say anything. Sometimes I think Samona scared the wits out of him, with her loud talk and wild manners. As for me, I wanted to ask her if that outfit glowed in the dark but I knew that was no way to get information out of her.

"What's a wake?" I asked when she finally reached us.

"Whatcha wanta know for?" Samona said, running her words together.

"I just do, okay?"

"Well, what for?"

Enrie interrupted us. "W-We have to go to a wake, Samona."

Samona put her hands on her hips in concern. "Well, who's gone to meet the Lord?"

"Matant Margaret," I answered, squinting so I could make out Samona's face over the glare of her clothes. I was glad to see her hair was back in cornrows instead of its fried hairdo from yesterday.

Samona's eyes bugged and her mouth dropped wide open. "And y'all are going to a real, bona fide wake?"

Enrie moved closer to me at Samona's reaction. "Yeah, is—is it bad?"

Samona nodded gravely. "And you don't even know what it is?"

"I got an idea," I mumbled, trying not to show how affected I was by Samona's tone of voice.

"A wake," Samona whispered to herself. "A real bona fide wake."

"What?" Enrie asked in a high-pitched squeal.

"Well . . ." Samona took a deep breath. "The reason I know what a wake is is on account of my aunt Delia's wake that Nigel and Anthony got to go to last year." Nigel and Anthony were Samona's older brothers.

"Your aunt Delia ain't dead! She did my mother's hair at the shop last week," I said, frowning.

"Course she ain't, 'cause of the wake. Anthony told me all about it. There's moaning and screaming and singing and everybody's wearing black. Anthony said they was all grieving so hard Aunt Delia just woke up and started banging on the coffin and screaming for somebody to let her out. We all got our time to die, and this wasn't hers. Anthony said it was a real good wake—'cause oftentimes the body just stays dead. That's why you gotta make arrangements for the funeral, just in case they don't wake up," Samona said, sighing and snapping her bubble gum.

Enrie's mouth dropped open. "Really, Samona?"

I let out a little laugh to show her that I wasn't scared. "Stop fooling around, Samona."

But Samona didn't smile one of her big grins or laugh or anything. She held up two fingers and crossed her heart. "That's what Anthony told me."

Then she turned around and skipped out of the schoolyard, her sweat suit getting dimmer and dimmer with each hop, leaving me and Enrie to stare at each other.

Morton's funeral home in Mattapan Square did not seem one bit like a place where a dead person would be waking up. In fact, it looked like the kind of house I wish we could live in. It was two stories high with big windows. It was painted white with black shutters and it even had a little green lawn with a white picket fence around it. That was on the outside.

Now I don't believe in superstitions or evil signs and all. Finding out Mrs. Fabiyi was no witch doctor had cured me of believing in anything that I didn't see with my own eyes. And I sure couldn't put much faith in anything Samona said. But when puffy clouds the color of wet cement started rolling in just as Papi was driving Jean-Claude and Chantal and me to the funeral home that night, and when lightning all of a sudden lit up the sky like firecrackers, even I had to believe it meant something.

I had been thinking hard about what Samona told me all day. I wanted to believe she was fooling, but

Samona would never cross her heart and lie at the same time. And come to think of it, I do remember her aunt Delia being very sick last year. Manmi and Granmè had gone to visit her in the hospital. And all day I was remembering that movie Enrie and me had seen last month about zombies that came alive and voodoo stuff. Manmi was so mad when I told her about it. She sat me down and tried to get me to see that the movie was just twisting stuff around and that the people who made the movie didn't know nothing about it in the first place. She said all that movie was about was distorting reality.

But this was for real. Maybe it's just me, but the way I figure it, if a body up and dies, they should make it their business to stay that way. Mrs. Whitmore was telling the class the other day that the world has a terrible population problem and that death was one of the few things that kept this problem from getting out of control. Then I started to feel bad 'cause I know how much Granmè loved her sister and I know how I would feel if Chantal died. I knew that I should pray real hard with everybody and hope that Matant Margaret would wake up and go back to the nursing home. But at the same time, I was not looking forward to this wake. Especially when I heard all the wailing before we even got up the steps.

I could hear a low moaning sound coming from behind the door. Jean-Claude had to push me up those stairs. It sounded like a pack of dogs howling and moaning in the middle of the night. I moved a little closer to Jean-Claude as the door opened up to a little hallway with a deep red carpet. At the same time, I heard a scream coming from somewhere inside. Maybe we'd missed the whole thing. Maybe Matant Margaret was jumping out of her coffin right now and walking around shaking people's hands!

"Seth." Jean-Claude looked down at me and I realized I was holding on to the edge of his dark blue suit jacket. He looked older in his suit and tie. He had even taken his earring out of his ear in respect to Granmè. She wouldn't talk to him for two weeks after he got his ear pierced. She kept saying that the next thing Jean-Claude would do is start wearing a dress. "Take it easy, man."

I let go of Jean-Claude's suit quickly. If Jean-Claude wasn't scared, then I wasn't gonna be scared either. Besides, what could happen with Papi and Manmi and the rest of the family there? I made up my mind to pray as hard as I could for Matant Margaret to wake up. I would even shake her hand if she wanted.

A short, fat man in a black suit came up to us and began talking to Papi. He had skin the color of peanut butter and a round bald head that looked like it had been greased to make it shine. He was shaking his head and talking very fast. I wondered if working here around all these dead bodies was what made his hair fall out, but I didn't think it would be appropriate to ask.

After a few minutes, we started to follow the bald man down the hallway with the red carpet. The closer we got, the louder the moaning became. I thought I could feel vibrations coming through the floor, like when someone is playing music too loud. The bald man led us all the way to the back of the house to a set of double doors. From all the noise slipping through the cracks under the door, it sounded like there was a circus going on in there. The bald man opened his mouth to say something, then just shook his head, pointed at the door and walked back down the hallway.

Papi turned to look down at the three of us. His eyebrows were close together and he had those wrinkles on his forehead. That meant he had something serious to tell us. We could tell he was trying to tell us to behave ourselves. Jean-Claude, Chantal and I nodded quietly. Then Papi reached out to open the door and he barely touched it before it flew open and all this rush of sound erupted from the room and filled the hallway, the entryway and the whole building.

I stepped inside the door behind Chantal and stared at what was going on in amazement. The room was full of relatives and family friends in black dresses and suits. There were wooden-back chairs all over the place and set up in no kind of order. There was singing going on in one corner and crying in another. Some people were sitting and talking, others were standing and laughing. I saw old Madame Germaine who used to give me candy to eat while we were in church and Alberthe with her big red cane and more of Granmè's friends sitting with two rows of old ladies weaving back and forth in their seats and making that terrible moaning sound I had heard from way outside the house. Behind them were three or four white-haired old men, including Ti Jacques, who was sitting with them rubbing his curly white beard. They had their heads hanging low and their feet stomping out a quiet and regular beat on the floor and they were humming all the while. I saw Tant Renee on her knees in the middle of a group of kneeling women leading a rosary chant. Tant Cherise was jumping out of her seat every couple of minutes and screaming *"Amwe!"* and falling to her knees and pulling her hair out. Manmi and Monnonk Roddie would pull her back up and sit her down and she would start all over again. And right in front of it all was Matant Margaret lying in a long, shiny casket with brass handles on the sides and flowers sitting all around it.

Papi led us through the maze of people and chairs to the front of the room where Manmi and Granmè were sitting. Manmi had her eyes closed and was singing something in Kreyol. Her dark hair had come loose from her scarf and was hanging down the sides of her face. Granmè was sitting very quiet and looking at the coffin in concentration. She didn't take her eyes off of it even when I leaned down to kiss her. But she felt for my hands, so I could tell she knew I was there. Way in the back of the room I noticed Jerome sitting in a corner. He'd dressed up in a suit too and was looking straight at Chantal. I hoped Jean-Claude didn't see him or this wake would get even louder.

I moved down the rows of chairs to sit next to Enrie. He was wearing a new gray suit and a blue and black tie. He was sitting way back in his chair and watching everything with round eyes. We looked at each other and I knew he was thinking the same thing I was: If this wake didn't get Matant Margaret up, nothing would. We sat back to wait.

All of a sudden, it got real quiet and still except for some low singing and the quiet stomping. One by one, people began to go up to the coffin and spend a few minutes looking at Matant Margaret. Some of the people had sad looks on their faces; some of them had tears dripping off their chins. Other people looked like they didn't know what to do, and didn't look straight in her face. It made me feel strange watching all of them. At the same time it made me feel peaceful, too. All those people really knew Matant Margaret. They had talked to her and played with her when they were as small as me. I didn't know her at all except from the stories about her. Granmè would tell us that Matant Margaret was the one who would suck the mango seeds dry and ran the fastest and told the funniest stories. If she wore her hair in three braids, the other girls would want to do the same. If she decided to play *kache kache li byen,* the rock-hiding game, everybody would want to play with her. It was Matant Margaret who went to America first. She saved all her money from working in the casinos and took a plane—not a boat, Granmè would make sure to tell us—to New York. Then she saved all her money working as a maid to bring Manmi and Tant Cherise. Then they all saved money to bring Monnonk Roddie, who was still little, and Granmè and Tant Renee. Granmè said the first thing Matant Margaret did when all of the family was in New York was quit her job as a maid and go to City College 'cause she figured it was time she did a little something for herself and let everyone else support *her* now. She was forty-eight years old when she got her nursing degree. Manmi always says that if it wasn't for Matant Margaret, she would never have met Papi in New York and they would never have gotten married and we would never have been born.

But I most remember the story that Granmè told me about Matant Margaret and their own grandfather—my gran-gran-granpapa. He was old and yellow when they were just little girls, Granmè had said. Everybody was saying he was losing his mind 'cause he took to mumbling to himself all the time and was making mistakes. He would go out fishing and come back with a goat or a chicken and swear until he cried that he had caught it in the sea. He would talk to the chairs and listen like they were going to talk back to him. He would get up and walk out of the house in the middle of dinner, thinking he had to go to work. Everybody except Matant Margaret would start laughing and talk about the old people's disease. It was Matant Margaret who would always go after Gran-gran-granpapa. She would catch up with him at the end of the road, take his hand and walk with him wherever he wanted to go. They would stop on the street and buy some *akara,* which is fried beans, or burnt plantain to eat from whoever was selling it on the side of the road. Then they would walk and walk and not go back home until it was dark and dinner was over. Granmè said that Matant Margaret was the only one who didn't cry when Gran-gran-granpapa finally died.

Thinking about that story, I knew I wasn't gonna be scared when it was my turn to look at Matant Margaret. I thought about how long she had been living in that nursing home and I knew—no matter what Samona said—that she wasn't going to wake up. For the first time, I started to feel sad about Matant Margaret dying.

When there was no one left but our two families, Enrie whispered to me that he figured Samona had been lying to us the whole time and all of a sudden, I didn't care. I would get Samona for making a fool of me tomorrow but for now, I wanted to think about Matant Margaret some more.

# CHAPTER

# 5

When Manmi asked me to bring some food over to Mrs. Gemini's the day after the funeral, I was glad to go. We had tons of food left over because everybody had come over to our apartment afterwards. *Grio,* which is fried pork; *du riz djon-djon,* which is rice and dried mushrooms; macaroni; cake—everybody brought something and our refrigerator was so full you couldn't open it up without something falling out.

Our apartment was still full of relatives, too, who came from New York, Miami, Canada and Haiti. Everybody came to say good-bye to Matant Margaret and to spend some time with Granmè. It was a real big deal now that she was the oldest living person in the family. Our apartment was so crowded that Jean-Claude and I had to sleep on the floor in the living room. And it gets very tiring having to kiss a whole roomful of relatives good morning and good night and hello all the time. What's really tiring, though, was all the noise. They spent all day arguing politics about Haiti and nobody agreed about anything except that Haiti is in bad shape and something has to be done about it. My cousins who live in Haiti said that gas has gotten so expensive that people are stealing it from other cars and there's no electricity at night. Ti Odette said that in Port-au-Prince, there are bodies found every day because the secret police are trying to put down any resistance to the Haitian army. It all sounds like a nightmare and I know that Manmi and Papi feel bad that they can't take us to Haiti in the summers like they used to. We haven't gone in five years so I don't even remember much about it.

Anyway, with all the noise at our apartment, going to Samona's house was like an escape. I was surprised when Chantal came into the kitchen and told Manmi that she would help me carry the food. Chantal had been busy with Marie and Rochelle, two of our cousins from Haiti. They'd never been to the United States and Chantal loved showing them around Boston.

Chantal hadn't gone with me to Mrs. Gemini's in a long time. She used to be good friends with Samona's big sister, Leticia, but they stopped hanging around together after Chantal started seeing so much of Jerome.

Jerome. That was it.

As soon as we got outside I stopped and turned to Chantal. "You're sneaking out to see Jerome, right?"

Chantal sighed and dug her hands into her jeans. "Don't tell Manmi or Papi."

We started walking down the street together. Chantal knew I wouldn't tell Manmi or Papi but I didn't like the way she was putting me in the middle of all of it. Suddenly I wanted to know what was so special about Jerome that Chantal would lie and sneak away for him.

"Why do you like Jerome so much?" I asked.

Chantal looked surprised. She searched my face for a minute. "You really want to know?"

"Yeah," I said, nodding.

"He listens to me, for one thing."

I frowned. "We listen to you too."

"No you don't." Chantal sucked her teeth. "Neither does Manmi or Papi. Jean-Claude used to listen to me when we were little but he's so busy playing street hero these days, he doesn't have time. You don't listen either, Seth. You think I'm just a little Manmi to take care of the house. You and Jean-Claude get attention for other things. I get good grades like you and Jean-Claude, but it doesn't count as much."

I thought about that. It was kinda true that I thought of Chantal as a little Manmi. We had never played together like Jean-Claude and I did when I was little. She was always with Manmi and Granmè learning how to cook, clean and sew.

"Do you mind doing all that stuff—the cooking and cleaning all the time?" I asked, thinking about all of Jerome's questions from the first time he had come over. Jean-Claude and I don't know how to cook any-thing. Neither does Papi.

Chantal shrugged. "I used to think it was unfair but whenever I said anything Manmi would start talking about American ideas going to my head. It's easier to just do it than fight about it all the time. All Manmi and Papi expect of me is to go to college and become a nurse and marry a good Haitian man."

I didn't see anything wrong with that but I didn't say anything. Chantal kicked a pebble along as we kept walking. I remembered that Samona once told the class that she wanted to be an astronaut and Mrs. Whitmore couldn't stop herself from laughing. Samona had been so mad, she'd gone home at lunch and brought her mother back to tell Mrs. Whitmore off. I had always thought that Chantal wanted to be a nurse too though I don't think I ever heard her say so. Maybe Chantal was right. Maybe we don't listen to her.

"Do you want to be an astronaut or something?" I was ready to listen.

Chantal laughed. "No. I don't want to be an astro-naut. And I don't want to be a nurse either. Being around all those sick people would make me just as sick. I'm not even sure I want to get married—ever!"

"Well, what do you want to be?"

Chantal searched my face again. "You really want to know?"

"Yeah." Of course I wanted to know.

"You remember anything about Haiti? All the summers we spent in Bonville?"

Bonville was where Manmi grew up. It's hard for me to remember much else. Haiti seems so far away most of the time. When Manmi and Papi tell stories about growing up there, it's hard for me to picture the places they talk about or the mountains they describe.

"A little," I said, trying harder to remember. "I remember Granmè killing chickens in the yard. And I remember Carnival—'cause we all dressed up in costumes and you had a long wig on."

"It was so beautiful." Chantal smiled. "Everything. You remember the markets? Granmè used to wake us up really early on Tuesdays to buy fish. Don't you remember the time we bought those live crabs and they got out of the box and you were screaming? You remember the Bouki and Ti Malice stories that Monsieur Lulu used to tell us in the dark?"

I could remember pieces of everything Chantal was saying, especially the storytelling. "I remember the story you told me about the *lougawou* that eats kids and I was so scared I wouldn't go outside at night for a whole week."

"Everything is such a mess now. You should hear the things Marie and Rochelle tell me. School is hardly ever open. I know that there were probably problems when we were there too but we were too young to know about them." Chantal sighed and stopped walking. "I want to help Haiti. Maybe go into government and

48

work for the United Nations. I don't know—Jerome thinks I can do it. Haiti even had a woman president for a little while—"

"You want to be president of Haiti?" I said. My sister? President of a whole country?

"No." Chantal shook her head. "But I could if I wanted to be."

I didn't know what to say. I was still in shock. Chantal had big dreams. It was hard to suddenly start thinking about her in a different way. She was looking at me like she wanted my permission or something but I didn't know what to say.

"Forget it." Chantal turned around and started walking the other way. "I'll see you later, Seth."

I watched her walk away before turning back toward Samona's house. I needed to talk to Jean-Claude about all of this. But right now I had to concentrate on Samona. I had to tell her off so she wouldn't think she'd actually scared me with her story about the wake. And if you can manage to put Samona aside and all, her house is fun to go to. There's always something different going on. The last time I had to go over there, Samona's brother Nigel had bought one of those kiddie pools and had everybody in it crushing grapes with their bare feet. He was trying to make the very first bottle of Gemini Wine. Nigel wants to be an inventor.

Samona's house sticks out from every other one on the block. It doesn't have grass, bushes or trees in front of it. Mrs. Gemini turned every inch of ground into a big vegetable and herb garden that goes all around the house. So when you're walking up the steps, instead of grass and flowers you can see corn, carrots, eggplants, rosemary, sage and other stuff growing out of the ground. Samona told me her mom has a big thing about organic food, which means food that's all natural and doesn't have pesticides or preservatives in it.

I didn't even bother knocking on the front door because nobody ever answers it. One time I stood out there for half an hour knocking and ringing before Leticia shouted out the window for me to stop making a racket and go through the basement door in the back of the house. I went straight there today and found Mrs. Gemini in the basement cutting pieces of cloth at her worktable.

"Young King," Mrs. Gemini said, looking over her glasses at me. "Long time no see."

Mrs. Gemini is very, very tall, almost as tall as Papi. She has a face shaped like a triangle and eyebrows that look like bird's wings.

"Hi, Mrs. Gemini," I said, putting the bag of food on the table beside her. Mrs. Gemini calls me Young King because she says I always look like I have the burden of a kingdom on my shoulders.

She shook her head, and about a million tiny braids fell out from whatever was holding them together at the top of her head. They looked like tiny snakes. "You got a number for me to play?"

"Mrs. Gemini," I said, shaking my head too, "you

know what the chances of you winning the lottery are?"

"Chances, shmances. I was born lucky, Young King. If I just focus my entire spiritual and mental being toward it—it will happen."

"You say that every week, Mrs. Gemini, and it still hasn't worked." I smiled at her. "What kind of a star did you say you were born under?"

She smiled and rubbed my head. "I need a kid like you to keep my feet planted in the earth. And how many times do I have to ask you to call me Binta, Young King? How go the affairs of statehood?"

I sat down in a chair next to Mrs. Gemini. No matter how much she asks me, I can't bring myself to call her Binta. It just doesn't seem proper. "Huh? You mean the funeral? Manmi sent over some of the leftover food for you. She said to thank you for the wreath."

"Good. Now I won't have to scavenge the garden for lunch." Mrs. Gemini went back to cutting the black and red striped cloth on the table. "Is everything okay at your place? Your grandmother feeling better?"

"I guess so. She got up to vacuum the house at six o'clock this morning. Woke everybody up," I said, trying to sound annoyed. Truth was, I was glad to hear the vacuum. That meant everything was back to normal.

"Good. Tell your manmi that I'll drive her to work Monday morning so we can do some woman-talk."

I watched Mrs. Gemini do her work for a minute,

then realized that she was cutting out numbers and arranging them in different combinations. She was obsessed. I looked behind her to see if her computer was on. "No poetry today?"

Mrs. Gemini sighed, and her braids shook a little. "Writer's block, Young King. Woke up with it. Looks like I'm going to have to call up *Intruder* for an assignment. I think they want me to do something religious next. Nation of Islam or something. Some ex-minister with a thing for loose women. Just as long as I don't have to impersonate a nun."

I laughed. The last thing Mrs. Gemini looked like was a nun. She does undercover assignments for the magazine *Intruder* to make extra money. Mrs. Gemini says you couldn't buy a whistle with the kind of money poets make. She's famous, though. She's always doing readings at the library and at colleges. One time PBS did a special on poets during the civil rights movement and the Black Power movement and they did a whole section on Mrs. Gemini.

"Well, Young King, I know you didn't come here to watch me cut numbers. Go on upstairs and make sure my children are keeping their activities within the guidelines of the living," Mrs. Gemini said, wiggling her eyebrows up and down. "I think Leticia has Samona taking calls from the psychic hot line."

"I really came to deliver some food," I said, starting up the stairs to the kitchen. I didn't want Mrs. Gemini thinking I came here *just* to see Samona.

There was nobody in the kitchen, but I could see why Mrs. Gemini was hiding out in the basement. Leticia was singing at the top of the lungs from somewhere in the house.

*"La, la, la, la, la, lahhhhh!"*

I put my hands over my ears and started to go into the family room, when I noticed a piece of paper pinned to the refrigerator door. It was Samona's application for the beauty contest, all filled out in red ink.

The Little Miss Dorchester contest is a junior beauty pageant held every year in our town. Since it's based mostly on looks, Samona was gonna turn some heads all the way around. Each year a bunch of stupid girls sign up to be in it, hoping to win the seventy-five-dollar check and the trophy and get their picture in the paper. I still didn't believe she would actually go through with it. Knowing her, she would probably forget to turn in the application on time.

Nigel, Anthony and Samona were in the family room, all of them talking at the same time. Samona was on the red phone which Leticia had installed for the hot line. Nigel and Anthony were sitting on the floor in front of the couch with what looked like all twenty-seven volumes of the Encyclopedia Americana around them.

*"I said, a tall dark stranger is coming into your life!"* Samona shouted into the phone, rolling her eyes at me. She had a stack of cards in front of her with things Leticia had told her to say.

I went over to Nigel and Anthony and sat down on the couch behind them. They were wearing the same football jerseys and sweatpants. They looked more like twins than brothers, except that Anthony had a scar on the right side of his face from a fight he got into a long time ago and Nigel was starting to grow a mustache. Nigel and Anthony are as different as you can get, though. Nigel likes to think. He's studying to be an engineer at Boston College and he spends all his time at his computer. But Anthony used to be a hood right after they first moved to Boston. He was in a gang and carried a gun and used to get into fights—that's where he got the scar. But all that changed after Anthony got sent to a home for juvenile delinquents for a few weeks. Last year he finished off his high school diploma and then began taking art classes at night. Anthony wants to be an architect. Jean-Claude said that the juvenile hall had helped to make Anthony take things more seriously.

*"When? Sometime soon!"* Samona shouted into the phone.

"I'm telling you, Tone, all the good things have already been invented. The airplane, the telephone, the whoopee cushion. Hi, Seth," Nigel said, throwing down Volume 7 of the encyclopedia.

*"I don't know what he'll look like exactly, lady! Isn't tall dark and handsome enough for you?"*

Leticia sang, *"La, la, la, la, lahhh!"*

"What are you guys looking for?" I asked, unstopping my ears. "What's Leticia doing?"

"Opera singing lesson," Anthony groaned, flopping down on his back. "She saw Leontyne Price on TV and now she thinks opera's going to be her life."

"Maybe *we* should watch TV. That's where Letty gets all her ideas," Nigel suggested. "She's made money off the hot line."

*"Fat? Lady, I promise you he won't be fat! He will be the one you have been waiting for."*

"What about the wine?" I asked.

"Now that was a good idea," Nigel said, rubbing his chin. "But a good wine takes years to develop its flavor."

"Huh?"

"We gotta store the wine in the basement for fifty years," Anthony said. "It don't taste like nothing but grape juice right now. But, man, our kids will make a fortune off of it."

*"La, la, la, la, lahhhh!"*

*"That's it, lady! Your time is up!"* Samona hung up the phone and unplugged it from the wall. "And that's it for me too. This hot line's out of business."

"We're searching for something with great creative potential," Nigel said, picking up another volume of the encyclopedia. "Something that will bear our name forever. Do you realize man has yet to land on Pluto?"

From the corner of my eye I could see Samona sneaking out of the family room.

"Something all natural—maybe we could use Ma's vegetables. I got it! A vegetable love potion." Nigel's eyes lit up.

"What? Man, that's stupid." Anthony shook his head. "This is all Ma's fault. Whenever she has writer's block, our creative juices get blocked too. It's a curse."

I followed Samona into the kitchen before she could disappear. "Wait a minute, Samona Gemini, I've got something to say to you!"

Samona had the nerve to look surprised. "I know you're not taking that tone of voice with me in *my* house."

"You lied to me and Enrie about the wake," I said, wagging a finger in her face. "I didn't believe you for a minute, but you scared Enrie."

Samona went to the refrigerator and pulled out a pitcher of some brown-colored stuff. "I didn't lie. Anthony *did* tell me that was what a wake was. He lied to me."

"Samona, you just can't go around lying to people," I said, very seriously. "It can get you in a lot of trouble—"

"Stop being such a stick-in-the-mud, Seth. I bet I made the wake a whole lot more fun for you and Enrie," Samona said. "Want some tannia juice?"

"What is it?" I asked suspiciously. "All that stuff about your aunt Delia too—what if I told her you were telling stories about her having a wake?"

"Aunt Delia wouldn't care." Samona poured out two glasses of juice. "It's root juice."

"No thank you." I pushed the glass away. "This isn't a social call, Samona. I came to set you straight. You can't just go around making up stories."

"Why not?" Samona asked, seriously.

"You'll get a terrible reputation. That's why I don't like to hang around you—"

"Okay," Nigel said, running into the kitchen with Anthony right behind him. "Put some pots on the stove, Samona, we're gonna cook up a love potion. And keep a lookout for Ma. She'll kill us if she sees us messing in her garden."

"A love potion." Samona wrinkled her nose. "That's stupid."

"That's what I said," Anthony grunted, following Nigel out the door. "Kid stuff."

"I want to dig, too!" Samona shouted, her eyes lighting up. She rushed out the door and looked back at me. "Come on, Seth."

I shook my head and glared at her instead. I was still mad at Samona, and I didn't think digging up Mrs. Gemini's garden was a good way to prove my point.

I sighed and got up to put the tannia juice back into

the refrigerator. Samona would never change. I didn't know why I even bothered to come over here. It was best to stick to my lifelong plan of avoiding her.

I went back down to the basement to say good-bye to Mrs. Gemini. She had finished cutting the cloth and was sewing different numbers together.

"Leaving so soon? Give me a hug, Young King." Mrs. Gemini opened her arms and hugged me. She smelled like all kinds of vegetables mixed together. "You know, Samona doesn't have many friends."

I started to tell Mrs. Gemini that Samona didn't have *any* friends but then I realized she thought *I* was Samona's friend. I decided not to break her heart.

"I think Samona would be a very lonely girl if it wasn't for you." Mrs. Gemini rubbed my head and let me go. "Thank you, Young King."

"Bye, Mrs. Gemini." I could feel my face getting hot. I hurried back outside, thinking about what Mrs. Gemini had said. Samona *doesn't* have any friends, I thought; she doesn't hang out with any of the girls in our class like Bessie Armstrong or Maisie Hong. That's because everybody thinks she's weird, I said to myself. From what I could tell Bessie Armstrong was the kind of girl who jumps rope and plays with dolls. Samona was the kind of girl who goes to a witch's house and gets banned from field trips for a whole school year. About the only girl stuff she ever seemed interested in was this beauty contest. If Samona would only dress normal and stop talking about weird things and act like every other girl, I thought, she'd be fine.

Papi was sitting on the steps of our apartment building when I got back home. He had on his red soccer uniform and was dripping with sweat.

"Did you beat the Saints?" I sat beside him. I wanted to talk to Papi about Samona and Chantal. But I couldn't talk about Chantal without getting her in trouble.

"Pulverized them." Papi kicked his leg out. "The Mighty Spiders keep spinning webs of victory."

"You sound like Mrs. Gemini's poetry."

"You just came from there, right? Spending some time with Samona? *Ki jan li yé?* How is she?" Papi asked, still smiling.

"It's not funny, Papi," I said seriously. "I keep trying to tell you that Samona's crazy. Why doesn't anyone believe me?"

"Samona's her own person." Papi pulled a towel out of his gym bag and wiped his face. "Very few people can say that at her age. You see all the time how kids are trying to copy each other's hair and clothes and style. Samona's comfortable with herself."

"Yeah, but nobody *else* is comfortable with her. She acts so different from everyone else. She's always making up these wild stories—"

"You should know about being different," Papi said. "Remember last year when you had that *ti neg ayisyen*

59

—the new Haitian boy in your class? The one that couldn't speak English—Marcel?"

"Marc." I nodded. "Nobody liked him just 'cause they couldn't talk to him. Samona helped me to teach him English."

"Different doesn't mean bad. It just means different," Papi said. "If Samona was like every other girl at school, would you notice her? If everybody had the same personality and behaved the same way then life would be very boring. Think about what life would be like with no Samona."

"Peaceful," I said.

Papi picked up the soccer ball and stood up. "Speaking of peace, let's not go upstairs yet. Do you want to help me practice some soccer kicks at the park?"

"Yeah," I said quickly, and he winked at me. All of the relatives were getting on his nerves too. I jumped up and followed Papi.

# CHAPTER

# 6

On Sunday, I woke up early 'cause Jean-Claude and Chantal were fighting again. It was a good thing the last of our relatives had gone home last night, 'cause they were yelling so loud they would have woken everybody up. Then I heard Manmi shouting at them and they got quiet fast. I rubbed my eyes and got out of bed 'cause there was no use going back to sleep now. We had to go to church every Sunday and I knew that soon Granmè would be knocking on the door telling me to get up and to go to my *twalèt*, which means "wash up!" I peeked through the blinds and saw it was raining outside. That meant we would drive to church. Manmi makes us walk when it's nice out 'cause the church is only five blocks away. It takes us forever to get there 'cause Granmè walks so slow.

I went to the closet to take out some of my only-wear-to-church clothes and I heard Jean-Claude slam into the room and throw himself on his bed. When I turned around, I saw that he was still in his blue-striped pajamas and he was beating his fist in the pillow. All of a sudden, he stopped and turned over and put his hands behind his head.

"Jerome again?" I said, not really expecting an answer. I wanted to talk to Jean-Claude about everything Chantal had said yesterday but I felt like I needed to talk to Chantal again just to make sure I had everything right. I was still having trouble understanding it all. Chantal didn't want to be a nurse, didn't want to do all the housework, didn't want to marry a nice Haitian man and could be president of Haiti if she wanted to. I knew if I told Jean-Claude just like that, he would think I was as crazy as Samona Gemini.

"Chantal doesn't know what's good for her. I could kill Jerome for all the trouble he's making for her," Jean-Claude said, his lips tight together.

"Shouldn't be too hard. He's shorter than you," I said, putting on my bathrobe and getting ready to go to the bathroom. "How are you gonna do it?" I didn't believe Jean-Claude for one second. He's always talking about how violence breeds violence and how black people need to stop beating each other up and stealing from each other. Jean-Claude would never do anything bad to another black person— even if they robbed him blind. He'd hunt them down and try to talk some sense into them. He always took the beggars on the street to get something to eat instead of giving them money so they wouldn't spend it on drugs or spirits.

Jean-Claude was quiet for a few minutes, then he sighed. "I have to go see Reggie."

Reggie? I frowned. "You don't mean that, right, Jean-Claude?" Reggie was this gang member who hung around Roxbury Heights. He was only sixteen years old but he was as tall as Jean-Claude and had a big build and everybody was scared of him. You didn't mess with Reggie. He'd been in jail twice already for stealing cars and holding up a store. People said he carried a gun with him all the time. Ever since he got out of jail the last time, he stayed out of trouble but made trouble for everybody else. Once in a while, Jean-Claude would go find Reggie and try to talk to him about the future and how he needed to change his ways. He even taught Reggie how to read. But it didn't help any. Reggie likes Jean-Claude a lot and respects him but he hasn't given up anything yet.

Jean-Claude didn't answer. He just kept his eyes shut and his hands behind his head. I went out into the hallway to find Chantal. Something must have happened for Jean-Claude to be talking about going to see Reggie.

I knew Papi was already at work and I could hear Manmi in the kitchen. She was listening to a mass on the Haitian radio station and singing along with the choir in Kreyol. I hoped Granmè was in there too 'cause I didn't feel like answering any of her morning questions. She asks me, Chantal and Jean-Claude every day if we brushed our teeth, combed our hair, put lotion on our face and legs and arms and if we prayed when we got up in the morning. She'll ask you those questions even if you're still in your pajamas and she knows you haven't even made it to the bathroom yet. Then she goes into our rooms to make sure we made the beds up 'cause we don't have any maids in this house and that's the first thing you do when you get up in the morning.

Chantal's door was closed. I put my ear against it but I couldn't hear anything. I knocked softly.

"Chantal, it's me."

I still didn't hear anything, so I tried the door. It was locked. I knocked again. "Chantal, I need to talk to you."

"Go away."

"Chantal, what's going on?" I asked as quietly as I could so Manmi couldn't hear me from the kitchen.

"Go away, Seth. It's none of your business." This time I heard Chantal's voice crack and I knew she must be crying.

"Please, Chantal, it's important," I started to say when I heard Jean-Claude coming out of our room. I turned around and I saw he was already dressed and was sneaking out the front door.

I ran up behind him just before the door shut. "Jean-Claude, where are you going? We gotta go to church—"

Jean-Claude pushed me back inside and held his

finger up to his lips. "Shhh! You don't know anything, okay? I've got some things I've got to take care of."

"Reggie?" I asked in a whisper. "And Jerome?"

"Yeah." Jean-Claude nodded. "Don't tell Manmi. You know she'll just get upset."

Then he ran down the hallway to the stairway entrance and was gone.

I closed the door and leaned against it. All I could think about was how Jean-Claude didn't like Jerome and how he was going to see Reggie. There was gonna be trouble. I ran back to Chantal's room and knocked on the door hard.

"Chantal, you gotta let me in—Jean-Claude's about to do something crazy," I said, breathing hard and fast.

After a couple of seconds I heard the lock turning, and then Chantal was standing in the doorway. Her eyes were red and her hair was all tangled up. She pulled me into the room and locked the door again.

I told her about what Jean-Claude had said about Reggie and how he had left all angry, and she just stood there, looking confused.

"What are you talking about, Seth? Jean-Claude would never kill anyone."

"That's what he said—"

"Why? That's crazy. He really said that? Maybe you misunderstood him, Seth."

Chantal looked even more upset than when I'd come in. "I don't know what's going on but you better find him, Seth. I need to talk to him about Jerome. I know I

**66**

can't keep sneaking around Manmi and Papi and I'm tired of fighting with Jean-Claude—"

Before I could ask any more questions, Granmè started banging on the door, promising to beat the person who'd locked her out of her own room.

I patted Chantal's shoulder again and unlocked the door.

Granmè burst into the room, already dressed for church and asking questions left and right. Why wasn't I dressed for church? Where was Jean-Claude? Why was the door locked? Why was Chantal crying?

"I have to get ready for church, Granmè," I said quickly. "Chantal doesn't feel so good. I don't think she can go to church. I don't know where Jean-Claude is." I backed out of the room.

I left before she could ask any more questions and hurried to the bathroom to take my shower. I had to think fast. I was remembering what Samona had told me once about wishing she had kept a better watch out for her brother Anthony. Even though she was just a little kid at the time, Samona thought she could have helped Anthony stay out of trouble. Reggie was trouble too and I knew I had to help Jean-Claude before he ended up like Anthony. If Jerome was working at 7-Eleven, that would mean Jean-Claude would need to get a ride there since it was off the highway. Reggie had a car but it would take Jean-Claude time to find him. Reggie was always in hiding just in case the police were looking for him. It usually took Jean-Claude a couple of hours to track Reggie down. That meant I had some time.

I kept thinking as I put on my clothes for church. I could hear Manmi and Granmè talking in the kitchen. They were upset because Jean-Claude had sneaked out of the house before church. Then I heard Manmi go down the hallway to Chantal's room and I knew she would be even more upset that Chantal wasn't going to church. I thought about sneaking out too but that would make everybody worry even more.

I stood in front of the mirror and brushed my hair. My face still looked dry so I put some more lotion on it automatically. I was glad my face didn't show how worried I was on the inside.

Manmi knocked on the door and came into the room. She looked real pretty all dressed up for church. She had on a long yellow dress and high heels so she looked taller. She came up behind me in the mirror and I could see the worry in her eyes.

"Seth, *Dou-dou,* what happened to Jean-Claude?" she asked quietly.

I looked away from her in the mirror and tried to think of what to tell her. I knew I couldn't lie to Manmi. She could always tell. But I couldn't tell her the truth either. "I don't know, Manmi. I saw him going out the door. He said he had to take care of something."

"You don't know where he was going?" Manmi's voice was soft with accents and concern.

68

I shook my head and I could see she could tell I wasn't telling the whole truth, so I decided to tell her a little more. "I think he went over to have one of his talks with Reggie."

Manmi looked relieved. "What about church? Jean-Claude and I are going to talk when he gets home. He may be a god out in those streets but in here he's a boy in trouble. Even God rests on Sunday."

I nodded and tried to smile.

"Are you ready? It's time to go." Manmi pushed me toward the door. "I am going to stay with Chantal and wait here for Jean-Claude. You go with Granmè. Ask her if she put anything into the food last night. There's something wrong with everybody in this house this morning."

It took us only five minutes to get to church. I was quiet the whole ride while I thought of what I could do. I couldn't get out of going to church but I could sneak out of Sunday school class and get back before the mass was over. I had to get over to the Zion Baptist Church where Samona's family went. The one person I knew who could find Reggie was Samona's brother Anthony, 'cause he used to be best friends with Reggie a long time ago.

I followed Granmè up the aisle when we got inside. We were early. Mrs. Volcy was playing the organ and the music filled the church. I looked at the altar. My friend Gerard and his older brother Patrick were going around lighting candles. They were dressed in the black and white robes that all the altar boys wear. I was glad Manmi wasn't with us 'cause she wants me to be an altar boy more than anything else in the world. Finally, I saw Enrie and Tant Cherise sitting in one of the pews. That was just what I was looking for.

I whispered to Granmè that I was going downstairs to the Sunday school class and that after that I would sit with Enrie for mass. I knew that she would be fine because she was sitting next to her friend Madame Germaine.

I went downstairs toward the church basement and went out one of the side doors instead. I stepped outside slowly. It was still drizzling. I wondered if God was going to strike me down for lying in church to Granmè and skipping out on the service to top it all off. But I had to find Jean-Claude. I had an hour and a half to get back before the service was over. I started running as fast as I could. I knew I could get to the Zion Baptist Church in fifteen minutes. And if everything turned out all right, I would go to confession and tell Father Dieujuste all about it.

# CHAPTER

## 7

The Zion Baptist Church was packed full. There were two rows of people who couldn't get seats just standing in the back near the doors. I didn't know how I was gonna find Samona and her family with all those people in there. I looked up at the front of the church. There was a big gospel choir sitting off to the side of the church in white robes. The other thing I noticed was that it sure was a lot noisier in this church than it was in St. Angela's. It was always real quiet in our church. You could hear every sneeze, every cough, and know who was getting whacked for not behaving. In this church there were people standing up and rocking side to side and calling out to the preacher. Everybody was fanning themselves and nodding. I could see the preacher standing in front of a microphone and waving his arms in the air. I stared at him for a minute before I realized what was different. It wasn't a him, it was a *her*. Girls can't be preachers—at least not in the Catholic Church. I was so surprised, I forgot about looking for Samona and started listening to the preacher instead.

"You've got to believe it in your heart. And yes, you've got to believe it in your souls! Look around you, my people, and see what I'm talking about!" The preacher was rocking back and forth, pointing here and there.

I followed one of the preacher's motions and found myself staring at Samona Gemini herself.

She was sitting halfway down the middle in a black dress and fanning herself. Leticia and Anthony were sitting beside her but I didn't see Nigel or Mrs. Gemini anywhere. Then I remembered they sang in the gospel choir.

I walked up the aisle as quick as I could, hoping no one would start thinking that I was there to testify or anything. Samona had told me about the testifying and getting saved that went on in Baptist churches. When I got to Samona's aisle, I pushed in and sat down right next to her.

"What are *you* doing here?" Samona whispered, crossing her arms in front of her and looking like she was going to take it upon herself to throw me out personally.

"Look, Samona, just be quiet and listen. Jean-Claude's in trouble," I said, then I spilled out the whole story to her in fast whispers.

Samona's eyes got bigger by the second and as soon

72

as I finished she was tugging on Anthony's sleeve and Leticia's dress and ordering them to follow her. Then she marched us right out of the Zion Baptist Church, right in front of everybody, with her chin up in the air like she was daring anybody to say something about it.

As soon as Leticia and Anthony knew what was going on, they both started talking at once.

"Seth, are you sure about this man? He said he wants to kill somebody? This doesn't sound like J.C." Anthony looked at me long and hard. I could see the scar on the side of his cheek standing out. He was dark like Samona, the same color as chocolate, but his scar was black.

"Chantal couldn't tell you if anything was wrong?" Leticia asked. She let out a long sigh and twirled one of her long braids. "This is crazy. Jean-Claude wouldn't snap like this. You know where you can find Reggie, Tone?"

Anthony nodded. "I got an idea. This all sounds too weird for Jean-Claude but if you're right, Seth, it could be too late already. I sure hope Jean-Claude keeps his cool until I can find him."

"I'm going with you," I said, without looking at either one of them. "He's my brother."

Anthony looked at me for a second and then nodded.

"You take the car. I'm going over to your house to check on Chantal," Leticia said, already walking away.

Anthony started walking toward his car but stopped when he saw Samona was following us. "Oh no, Samona. You're not going anywhere."

"I'm going with you," Samona said, opening her mouth for the first time since we stepped outside.

"Naw—you're not," Anthony snorted. "Where I'm goin' ain't no place for little girls."

"Good. 'Cause ain't no little girls here," Samona snapped back, putting her hands on her hips. She was making that face that meant there was no use arguing with her.

Anthony sighed, then shrugged his shoulders. I could see he was trying not to smile. "Fine. But you stayin' in the car—with Seth."

Samona and I looked at each other and nodded. It was better than nothing. The only person who could help me find Jean-Claude was Anthony.

Both of us got into the front seat of Anthony's red sports car.

"Where are we going?" Samona asked when Anthony started driving.

"Close to Field's corner, over by the old movie theater," Anthony said. He was racing the car down Blue Hill Avenue. I knew Papi would kill me if he knew I was in a car driving this fast with Anthony. "Last I hear, Reggie was staying with this honey he was seeing, Monique."

After a few minutes, Anthony finally slowed down

and parked. "Y'all are gonna stay in the car until I come back out."

Samona and I shook our heads and looked out the window. Anthony had parked on the street in front of an old brick building. It looked like it used to be an apartment building but all the windows were broken and there was trash all over the sidewalk. It was a dump.

Samona and I watched Anthony walk up the stairs and go inside.

"Maybe Jean-Claude's still there," Samona said.

"Maybe." I shrugged, trying to act like I wasn't worried. I turned my head back to watch the building some more. Maybe Jean-Claude hadn't even gotten there yet. I looked up and down the street, hoping to see him.

"Wait," I heard Samona say. She was looking across the street. "That's Reggie over there!"

I turned around fast and saw Reggie going down the alley next to the house across the street. It had to be Reggie. Nobody else would be wearing that long black leather coat and purple hat. "Let's go."

I jumped out of the car and ran across the street. I could hear Samona following me. Her church shoes were making a clack-clack sound every time they hit the ground. I turned my head to tell her to be quiet 'cause anybody could be in that alley, but I was too late.

"Reggieeee!" Samona started shouting when we reached the alley.

I saw Reggie turn around real fast and pull something out of his pocket. It was a gun. And he was aiming it straight at Samona and me.

I stopped running and started to put my hands up but Samona crashed right into me and both of us fell on the ground in a puddle of water.

"Hey, don't shoot them, man!"

I looked up and saw Anthony standing behind us, with his hands in the air.

"Tone, man." Reggie put the gun back in his pocket and waved Anthony over to him. Anthony walked around Samona and me. Then the two of them hugged.

"These two kids who you hangin' with these days?" Reggie asked, looking down at us.

I was staring so hard at Reggie, I didn't even bother to get up. I'd never seen him up close before. Everybody knows he's always wearing that purple hat and that long leather jacket but no one ever says anything about what he looks like. I was surprised.

Reggie was fat.

He had a big, puffy, moon-shaped face and the rest of him was puffy too. And he was real light-skinned. He was that almost white kinda black where you wouldn't be able to tell except for his hair and his mustache. He didn't look scary at all.

"Naw, G, that's my baby sister and Seth, J.C.'s little

brother," Anthony said. "We're lookin' for J.C. If these kids don't get themselves killed first."

I stood up finally and glared as hard as I could at Samona. She was trying to squeeze the water out of her black dress. Of all the stupid, crazy things that girl had gotten me into, this was the worst. She almost got us killed, running down the alley shouting Reggie's name like that.

Samona looked like she was going to say something but I stared at her even harder. "Just be quiet, Samona."

I turned back to face Anthony and Reggie again, half-expecting Samona to grab me by the neck for telling her to be quiet. But she just got up and came to stand beside me.

"He went looking for Jerome," Reggie was saying. "Came by about half an hour ago to give me a reading lesson but I had some business to take care of first."

Anthony shook his head. "Where'd he go after that?"

"I told him to sit down and chill while I was gone. But when I got back from my errand, he'd bummed a ride with Mace to the 7-Eleven to find Jerome." Reggie scratched his forehead. "What'd Jerome do? Thought he was flying straight like you. Don't tell me J.C. the savior's got another case on his hands."

Anthony shrugged. "Don't know for sure. But Seth's worried. Thanks, G, we gotta find him. Check you later."

"No you won't. J.C. done saved you," Reggie said.

He tapped Anthony on the arm and started walking back down the alley.

"Y'all don't listen too good," Anthony said when we got back in the car. "Or maybe I wasn't speaking the right language. I thought I said to wait in the car. You tell me. What does this sound like to you, Seth—'Stay in the car'?"

"Sounds like stay in the car," I mumbled. We were on the highway already, heading for the 7-Eleven. I was feeling better but I was still confused. Jean-Claude had gone to see Reggie about a reading lesson, not to get in any trouble. But what did he want to see Jerome about? It didn't make any sense.

"What's it sound like to you, Samona?" Anthony asked. He was still mad that we didn't follow his instructions.

Samona didn't say anything.

"Sounds like a death wish to me." Anthony smiled. "Wait till I tell Mama how you almost got yourself shot."

Samona was still silent and I looked over to see if she was okay. Just for a second, it seemed like Samona actually felt sorry or scared or something. Then she and Anthony started going at it like they always do. Samona fights with her brothers and sister a lot but it's not like when Jean-Claude and Chantal fight. Samona's family fight like they're playing most of the time. Jean-Claude and Chantal never used to fight about anything until Jerome came along.

I looked out at the highway again, glad that we were traveling so fast. I had to be back in church in half an hour.

"Look, there's Jean-Claude!" Samona shouted, pounding on my arm. We were pulling into the 7-Eleven parking lot. I looked out the window and saw Jean-Claude sitting in front of the store. He had his head in his hands and was all hunched over, like he was crying.

I jumped out of the car as soon as Anthony stopped it.

"Jean-Claude," I said, pushing his shoulder a little. I heard Anthony dragging Samona into the 7-Eleven.

"Jean-Claude," I said again, sitting down beside him. He was wet from sitting out in the rain. "You didn't do anything bad, did you?"

Jean-Claude lifted his head finally and looked at me. He wasn't crying at all but he did look upset. "What are you doing here, Seth?"

"I came to find you," I said, looking away. I looked up at the big green and red 7-Eleven sign, wondering what to say. I'd already made one mistake about Reggie. How could I tell Jean-Claude that I thought he was going to get into trouble over Jerome? Then I felt Jean-Claude put his arm around me.

"No blood. No police. And Jerome gave me this Slurpee for free," Samona announced, skipping out of the 7-Eleven with a big cup in her hand.

"And my man sitting outside in the rain." Anthony sat down with us. "What happened, J.C.?"

Jean-Claude swallowed. "I wanted to teach Jerome a lesson. Ever since he met Chantal she hardly talks to anyone anymore. She sneaks around behind Manmi and Papi's back. Last night she didn't come home until one in the morning and I had to cover for her. I had enough. I had to find out what was going on between them."

"But he wasn't here?" Anthony guessed.

"Naw—he—he was here." Jean-Claude sighed and clenched his hands. "I started looking in his face . . . and I knew I couldn't hit him. He wasn't worth it."

"What happened?" Anthony asked again.

"We talked." Jean-Claude shrugged. "I listened to all the stuff he was saying about us not treating Chantal the way we should and how she feels and . . . I realized he does care for her. He was telling me stuff I should have already known about Chantal."

Anthony was smiling wide and happy. "I knew you wouldn't let us down."

"I mean what's all my talk for if I can't live up to it?" Jean-Claude was shaking his head slowly.

"You didn't hit him? Once?" Samona asked, sipping on her Slurpee with a big sucking noise.

"Well." Jean-Claude stood up, pulling me with him. "Thinking about it was just as bad, Samona."

Anthony and Samona were laughing as we walked

back to the car, but Jean-Claude wasn't. He was serious and he meant every word he was saying. I wasn't laughing either. I was glad Jerome was okay. And I was glad Jean-Claude was okay too. Half the time I have to tune Jean-Claude out when he's talking about how black people gotta unify and be strong and going on and on about what black person invented this and that. Sometimes it feels like I'm in school with him talking and talking. But today I understood what he was trying to do. He was trying to make sure I grew up proud. He was trying to teach me everything they didn't teach at school and not to believe everything you see on television and movies that doesn't show the good side of being black. I was glad, when it came down to the line, all that talk was about real life—not just talk. I'd never thought about it much before, but I had a lot of respect for Jean-Claude.

But at the same time, I was kind of mad at him. Maybe what everybody says is right and I am too serious and that's part of the reason why I jumped to all these wrong conclusions this morning about Jean-Claude, Reggie and Jerome, but it was part Jean-Claude's fault too. Jean-Claude thinks he knows what's best for everybody. He tries to change people and usually it's for the better, but he was wrong about Jerome and Chantal. They didn't need changing. It was Jean-Claude who needed to do some listening. It was the first time I'd ever thought about Jean-Claude in this way.

"Seth," Samona said, bringing me out of my thoughts. I turned to look at her and was surprised at how serious she looked. "Are you mad 'cause I almost got us killed?"

"Yeah," I said. "This is exactly what I was talking about before, Samona. You finally got us into too much trouble."

"I'm sorry."

"You are?" I'd never heard Samona apologize about anything. I started to feel bad all of a sudden. It wasn't *all* her fault that we almost got killed. I was the one who jumped out of the car first. I was the one made us go look for Reggie. Samona had just been trying to help. I'm always going on and on to Samona about how crazy she is and how much trouble she's gotten me into but I had gotten us into the most serious trouble of all. Was I being like Jean-Claude? I didn't know how to tell Samona all of this without it going to her head. She looked like she was thinking hard about something else anyway.

"I'll see you at home," Jean-Claude said as we got back to church. "I'm sorry I made you worry about me like that."

"That's okay." I shrugged.

"No it's not," Jean-Claude said. "This thing has gone way too far. I'm gonna have a long talk with Chantal."

I had to move fast 'cause people were starting to come out of the church doors. I smiled back at Jean-

Claude, then stepped out of the car fast. "Thanks, Anthony—and you too, Samona."

The car drove off just in time. Granmè came down the steps of the church. I grabbed her hand.

When we got home, Chantal and Jean-Claude were in the kitchen talking.

"What's going on?" I asked.

Jean-Claude and Chantal smiled at each other.

"Get ready for fireworks, Seth," Chantal said. "I'm gonna tell Manmi and Papi about Jerome. And everything about how I feel too."

"Good," I said, seriously. " 'Cause honesty—"

Chantal grabbed me and gave me a kiss on the cheek. "Thanks for looking out for us, little brother."

# CHAPTER

# 8

Manmi grounded me for two days when she finally found out about me missing my piano lesson to go fool around at Mrs. Fabiyi's house. Mrs. Marshall, the piano teacher, always called the parents when a student didn't show up for a class. She said it was just in case one of us got kidnapped or murdered but I knew she was just trying to make sure she got paid anyway. I wasn't lonely though, 'cause both Jean-Claude and Chantal were on punishment for the rest of their lives so nobody could leave the apartment. Manmi and Papi kept looking at us like they didn't know who their children were— especially Chantal. They listened to all her feelings and they didn't say anything about American ideas but they didn't tell her she could stop cooking either. They're still thinking everything she said through. I think Papi understands about Chantal's dreams because of his dreams of being a pilot. Granmè agreed with Chantal one hundred percent and made Jean-Claude and me clean the bathroom this morning. It wasn't so bad.

While I was sitting at home those two days, I had plenty of time to think about Samona entering that beauty contest. It would never work. The more I thought about it, the funnier it became. It got to the point that at any moment, no matter where I was, I would bust out giggling.

The girls in the contest are judged on talent, personality and aptitude—most of which aren't Samona's strong points. Why, people run the other way when they see Samona coming. As for talent, Samona sings like a frog and still does dances like the funky chicken—on purpose.

Aptitude is about the only thing Samona does have. She's at the head of our class in everything. That makes our teacher, Mrs. Whitmore, mad 'cause she doesn't like Samona. The other thing is that it isn't obvious that Samona is smart. I mean, it doesn't show. They weren't going to be handing out tests at that contest, they were gonna be asking questions. As far as I could see, Samona didn't have a chance of winning that contest. No use telling my family that, though.

"Okay, Seth, what's so funny?" Papi said after I had started laughing while I had some red beans in my mouth at dinner the first night I was grounded.

Granmè told everyone that I had been doing this all day and felt my forehead to make sure I didn't have a fever.

"Don't pay him any mind," Chantal muttered. She was in a bad mood. Manmi and Papi had said she still couldn't have a boyfriend. And when she went food shopping with Manmi or walked to church with the family, Manmi watched her like a hawk.

"Like sister, like brother," Jean-Claude added, seriously.

Chantal stuck her tongue out at him. "I wouldn't talk, *Di-di.*"

Jean-Claude gave her one of his looks to kill. *Di-di* used to be his nickname when he was little, and he hated it. When he first went to high school, he made everybody promise not to call him that anymore. Everybody did except for Granmè. She laughed at him and said he must think he's something special. Everybody who's Haitian gets a nickname when they're a baby. Half our relatives still call me *Bou-bou* and Chantal *Chou-chou* from when we were little. Jean-Claude just gives them a look and they smile and call him by his given name. One time Samona heard Tant Renee call me *Bou-bou* and she just about burst a lung from laughing so hard.

"*Sa sifi,*" said Manmi quietly, which means "that's enough." "Now what is funny, Seth? God knows we need something to laugh about in this place."

I shrugged my shoulders. "Nothing, I guess. Samona says she's gonna be in that Little Miss Dorchester contest."

Chantal lit up like a firecracker. "She is? Well, all right. It's about time somebody with real talent entered that contest."

*"Vraiment?"* Manmi smiled. "We will have to go see it this year."

*"Lap gen siksè."* Granmè nodded.

I stopped taking bites out of my corn on the cob and looked at Granmè. "Win? Granmè, Samona's not going to win that contest."

Papi tapped my head lightly. "You don't know that, Seth. Samona has a good shot, just like the rest of those girls."

Jean-Claude snorted. "Yeah, right, Papi. She has about as much chance as a monkey. Some light-skinned, long-haired little girl that conforms to the judges' twisted concepts of beautiful will win as usual. When people say 'Black Is Beautiful,' they usually mean the brighter the black the more beautiful."

While I always think it's interesting to hear Jean-Claude's side of it, he was missing the point. All of them were missing the point.

"Black may be beautiful, y'all, but Samona ain't," I said finally.

I wished I hadn't said anything 'cause then through the rest of dinner I had to sit and listen to Manmi, Granmè and Chantal raving over Samona's big brown eyes and skin the color of maple syrup. None of them mentioned the way she dresses or the things she says. Samona's got this family hoodwinked. Then I thought about what had happened yesterday. I may have gotten us into some trouble yesterday but it was worth it because now there were no more secrets and not as much fighting. Samona had helped me when I needed to find Jean-Claude. It was my turn to help her out. She needed to see that this contest was a stupid idea. Samona was just gonna embarrass herself in front of everybody.

When I got to school on Monday, I was hoping that I could find out why Samona wanted to enter the contest so I could talk her out of it. I caught sight of her standing on the other side of the classroom in a pair of red overalls, and started to go over there when Bessie Armstrong tapped me on the arm.

For a minute, I didn't know what to say. Bessie Armstrong never spoke to anybody—especially boys. She had long, light brown hair that she always wore in two fat curls on each side of her head. She was so light-skinned she was almost white. This was on account of the fact that her father is white. She never acted up or yelled like the other kids in class did either. She sat there and "yes" and "no" as quiet as could be.

"Yeah?" I asked finally.

"Did you really go inside Mrs. Fabiyi's house like Samona said?" Bessie whispered.

"Sure did." I shook my head hard and long. Bessie was staring at me like I was Michael Jordan or something. For once I didn't mind Samona's bragging mouth.

"Was there bats in the corner of the room like Samona said? Did she really have a snake wrapped around her shoulders? How'd you get her not to eat you?"

I should have known. Samona had made up a story rather than admit the boring truth. Luckily, Mrs. Whitmore came in and saved me the trouble of having to answer.

"You sure are brave, Seth," Bessie whispered before going back to her seat.

I smiled and went to sit down at my desk in the back. Teachers always put me in the back 'cause I'm tall for my age but right then, I wished I was a little closer to Bessie, who was three seats ahead of me.

Mrs. Whitmore was doing roll call. I could see her sigh when she said Samona's name. I kinda felt sorry for her. Mrs. Whitmore is the kind of teacher who doesn't appreciate an imaginative person. Samona just about drives her crazy; Samona can get her so mad that you can see the skin hanging off Mrs. Whitmore's fat brown arms shake and jiggle and her eyes blink like crazy behind her black owl glasses. Mrs. Whitmore loves Bessie Armstrong.

It wasn't until the end of the day that I had a chance to talk to Samona. I found her in the yard showing a piece of paper to Bessie Armstrong. Bessie walked away looking confused, and I hurried over to Samona.

"Now, Samona, why do you want to go and bother Bessie Armstrong?" I asked.

Samona raised her eyebrows. "What's it to you? You got something for that girl?"

91

I glared at her real hard. The last thing I wanted to do was give Samona the impression that I liked Bessie. I'd never hear the end of it. Besides, I don't like *any* girls.

"Okay, okay, don't get an attitude," Samona sniffed. "Not that it's any of your business, but I was asking her if she wanted to practice for the contest together. I thought she could help me. Do you know she's been in the contest for the past three years?"

I stared at the white piece of paper in Samona's hand. There it was, her official entry form, stamped and everything. "Well, I guess you've gone and done it now."

"I told you I would."

I shook my head. "Samona, why do you want to enter that old contest anyway? There's no way you're gonna win."

"I got my reasons." Samona lowered her eyes. "Who says I'm not gonna win?"

"My brother, for one. He said there ain't no way those judges are gonna vote for you 'cause they're all mixed up about beauty anyway." I hoped this would make her change her mind. Samona loves to hear Jean-Claude talk. She thinks he's better than the church preachers. "Besides, you don't have any of the right qualifications."

Samona scratched her head and squinted her eyes. "Jean-Claude said I shouldn't enter the contest?"

I looked down at the ground. "No. He just said you're not gonna win. Same thing."

"But what's he think about me being in the contest?"

I sighed. "He said you got guts."

Samona lit up. "See? I'm doing the right thing. Besides, I already told Bessie I'd be in it. This contest is going to change my life. You'll see."

Now that was a funny thing to say. Since when did Samona care about Bessie Armstrong, who she never even talked to before today? And what did she mean the contest was gonna change her life?

"Well, seeing as you're going to go through with this, Manmi, Chantal and Granmè said if there was anything you wanted help with that you should come right over. Though I don't know what they think they can do."

Samona scowled and turned away. I walked toward the other end of the schoolyard, where my friend Skid was shooting hoops.

I played basketball with Skid as long as I could after school so I wouldn't have to go home, in case Samona was there. It didn't work, though, 'cause me and Skid got into a fight over who was going to get into the NBA first. Anybody could see that wasn't going to happen for Skid, 'cause both of his parents are real short and he's not likely to grow over five foot three.

"Na-uh." Skid shook his head violently. "No way, Seth. I'm a be six foot two at least. I'm gonna be just like Sweet."

I shook my head too. Sweet was Madison High School's star forward. He was so good, he already had NBA recruiters watching his game. He lived around the corner from me. But Sweet was six foot four. "Man, you'll be lucky if you make five foot one. You've been sitting in the front of the class since first grade."

Skid's face scrunched up something awful. His eyes narrowed and wrinkles appeared all over his golden-colored skin. He just can't stand to be told he's short. "Least I can shoot."

My mouth fell open. "What?"

"Yeah, that's right." Skid picked up the ball and tucked it under his arm. "You can't shoot and this is my ball and I don't play with people who can't shoot."

"Skid, I was only kidding," I said as he left. I felt sorry I had said anything at all now, not because Skid was mad—I knew he would forgive me—but because now I would have to go home.

I walked as slowly as I could, stopping at the corner to buy some gum and looking around to see if there was anyone hanging around at the community center. I saw Sweet there but he wasn't playing any ball, he was talking to some girl. Probably putting the moves on her. Disgusting.

When I finally got home, it was worse than I thought. There were pink and green rollers all over the place. Manmi's hot combs were sitting on the stove. I could smell grease, perfume and makeup in the air.

I found Jean-Claude hiding in the bedroom, reading the newspaper.

"Is she gone yet?" I asked, sticking my head in the door.

He shook his head disapprovingly. "They're in Chantal's room, making her as fake as they can."

I was just about to join him when Granmè grabbed me by the arm and began steering me to the room she and Chantal share. "That's okay, Granmè. I don't need to see her."

Granmè was shaking her head like she was upset. In the room Manmi and Chantal were standing in front of the mirror on the closet door and looking as if the world had taken a lot out of them. There was also some strange girl standing in between them.

It never entered my head that this girl was Samona. Samona didn't have no long, curly hair like that. Samona wouldn't be caught dead in a frilly yellow dress. This girl wasn't half-bad. This girl was almost pretty.

Before I could tell Manmi they had done up the wrong person, this girl marched up to me and whispered, "What are you staring at, bo-bo head?"

They had put a weave in Samona's hair and piled it up on top of her head, dressed her up like a regular person and caked makeup on her face, but they couldn't change the way she talked. And as long as she said things like that, Samona was not going to win that contest. Still, I couldn't help staring.

Samona leaned toward me again and I almost choked on the smell of her perfume. "If you say I look stupid, I'll lay you out, Seth Michelin."

I blinked and kept staring. "You don't look stupid."

In fact, she looked right nice, but I couldn't shake the feeling that something was wrong. She looked like any other eleven-year-old girl, I guess. What she didn't look like was Samona, and though I may be sick in the head, I wasn't sure I liked it. If they could change her on the outside so that she didn't look like Samona, maybe they could change her on the inside so she didn't act like Samona. Crazy as that girl is, I liked her better than the one standing in front of me.

"Well?" Chantal asked, looking like she didn't know what to say. "She asked for it."

I looked around the room and I could see that Manmi, Chantal and Granmè were all pretty horrified at what they'd done. I can understand why, seeing as they were Samona's biggest fans when she looked like her normal self. Normal. I never thought of Samona as looking normal before. I remembered what Mrs. Gemini had said about Samona being lonely and this time I started to take it seriously. Maybe Samona was tired of being weird. Maybe she was finally taking my advice and was trying to turn herself into a normal girl so she could have friends and jump rope and be just like all the other girls at school.

It was a scary thought.

97

# CHAPTER

# 9

Well, like it or not, it looked like I was gonna have to go to the Little Miss Dorchester pageant. Samona came over to our apartment peddling tickets and Manmi bought one for everyone in the family, then hung them up on the refrigerator so I had to be reminded of it whenever I went into the kitchen. I tried to prepare my family for the worst but they still thought Samona could win this contest even though they didn't approve of the new Samona's looks. They kept going on and on about how we had to show Samona how much we supported her and how Samona was so smart and so talented. They just don't know Samona like I do. Weave or no weave, she was just as likely to get up on the stage and do her favorite imitation of James Brown singing "Superbad" and jump around the stage like a chicken with its head cut off.

At least, that's what I thought at first. But after watching Samona for a couple of days, I wasn't so sure anymore.

She went and sold tickets to everybody at school before I could stop her. People just couldn't get over the new Samona. Before they had time to close their mouths and come out of shock, she had a ticket sold to them and a dollar in her hand. Even Mrs. Whitmore bought one. That isn't all. Samona was never around anymore, and she was acting funny. She was always running over Mrs. Fabiyi's after school to do some mysterious stuff or hanging out with Bessie Armstrong, of all people. Ever since that afternoon in the school-yard, they were always together at recess or at lunch giggling and whispering and practicing for the contest. They were also wearing the same color dresses to school and doing their hair the same way. The more I watched the two of them hanging around together, the more I realized Samona *was* changing. For one thing, I didn't have to try to avoid her these days. She hadn't come around to bother me at all. One time I went over to her house and Leticia told me she was over at Bessie's.

A few days before the contest, I caught Samona alone at the end of lunch period. I wanted to talk to her 'cause I was feeling like this change was kind of my fault—a little. Maybe I was as wrong about Samona as Jean-Claude had been about Jerome. I was the one who was always telling her how crazy she was and trying to get her to act normal like everybody else.

But all Samona could talk about was Bessie Armstrong.

"I like Bessie," Samona was saying, like she was surprised. "I wasn't sure I was gonna 'cause she's such a Miss Perfect Thang at school and doesn't even know how to laugh like when the map fell on Mrs. Whitmore's head. But then I started watching her and she doesn't have any friends."

I thought about that. Bessie spends all the class breaks and lunch period reading or studying. She sits in the front of the class where you can't even talk to the person next to you. And she always walks home from school alone. Samona was right.

"And she has a *terrible* home life," Samona continued, looking very concerned.

"What do you mean?"

"There's no brothers or sisters—not one. She has a lot of toys and a hundred dolls but her mama doesn't work so she's home *all* the time and she doesn't like noise. So Bessie always has to play real quiet and how are you supposed to get away with anything if your mama's home all the time?" Samona lifted her shoulders. "I don't like her house. There's no fun allowed there."

That did sound like a terrible home life.

"I guess everybody's different," I said, hoping Samona would get the point.

Then the bell rang and we had to go back to class.

On the day before the contest, I decided to go visit Mrs. Fabiyi and see if I could find out why Samona was spending all her time over there. I wasn't used to not knowing what's going on with Samona.

I heard Mrs. Fabiyi shouting, "Come in! You are welcome!" before I even knocked on her black door. I pushed it open and stepped through those slimy glass bead curtains. Mrs. Fabiyi was sitting on the floor in her living room wearing a bright yellow and blue cloth around her body and another head wrap made of the same material.

"Is that what they wear in Nigeria?" I asked, staring at her outfit. I hope she didn't give Samona any ideas about dressing like that. Samona already dressed weird enough—or she used to anyway.

"Humph." She looked at me for such a long time that I thought I could feel her eyes on my face. "Ah-ah, Seth. Is you. This? This you call *iro* in Yoruba—that is the language of my father's people. You wear the *iro* with a *bubba*—a shirt—but I like to be different. *Bubba* and *iro,* can you say that? No, please do not try. You only make sounds that hurt my ears."

"Booba and eero," I said, trying to make it singsongy like Mrs. Fabiyi had made it sound.

Mrs. Fabiyi shook her head and grimaced. "Please. What you come here for? No Samona with you today?"

"No." I shook my head and looked around. I guess that meant Samona hadn't come here today.

Mrs. Fabiyi looked at me for a long time again and

then began walking to the kitchen. "You want to know more about Nigeria, you drink my cassava. Come."

I followed her into the kitchen and sat at the small, round table while she heated some water on the stove. On the table, there were two long rectangular pieces of wood that looked like two thick paddles on top of each other. The top was carved into the figure of a big fish.

Mrs. Fabiyi sat down at the table with two big steaming mugs. "This game: *Ayo*. You open it and see game. Samona like to play all the time. All the time she asking me to play *Ayo*. So when she come I just say, Go into kitchen, little black American girl, and do not bother me."

I noticed that Mrs. Fabiyi called Samona a black American just like my parents do instead of using African-American like they tell you to in school. Jean-Claude said it was because black people have gone through so many name changes and African-American is just the latest one. Not everybody's caught up with it yet. Papi said it's because black people outside the United States don't think of black people here as Africans—just like he doesn't call himself African-Haitian even though all black Haitians are originally from Africa.

I moved the string that was holding the two paddles together and opened it. One of the pieces of wood flipped back and I could see that they were connected together. On each side were two rows of five holes, and in the last two holes were a bunch of marble-sized green balls that looked like beans.

"You drink." Mrs. Fabiyi pushed the game away and put one of the mugs under my nose. I looked into it and wrinkled my nose. There was some grainy white stuff mixed with hot water in the cup. It looked a little like grits. Manmi always tells us that we have to eat what's offered to us 'cause it's rude not to, but there was no way I was gonna drink this. Who knows what could be in it? What if some of that stuff about Mrs. Fabiyi being a witch was partly true? She did tell Samona that cats taste like chicken. I pretended to take a sip out of the cup and looked up.

Mrs. Fabiyi laughed and moved her head up and down like a yo-yo. "You not come here to drink cassava, eh? You come to talk Samona. I give her *Ayo* game tomorrow when she win."

Oh, boy. Another person who thought Samona was gonna win. I frowned and stared down at the *Ayo* game. Suddenly, I wished Samona had never even heard of this contest. I know the whole idea came as one of her stories to me and she just got stuck in it. Yesterday was one of the first real conversations Samona and I had where I wasn't trying to get away from her and she wasn't telling one of her stories. I used to think Samona told stories just to keep me from going away. Now it seemed like she didn't need to do that anymore. And with Bessie, she finally had a real friend. But everybody thought I was Samona's friend, too. Was I? I'd always told myself she was just Samona and I was just me. I thought I knew everything about her, until she changed. I guess the old Samona and I *were* kind of like friends. But would Samona go back to being herself after the contest?

"Mrs. Fabiyi, how does Samona look to you?"

"Ah!" Mrs. Fabiyi smiled, and I could see her shiny white teeth. "Samona look like her doll now. Pretty doll. She think she like play doll. New hair. New dress. New game. New Samona."

"That's what I'm afraid of," I mumbled.

"Afraid? What afraid for? Samona make some good change, some bad. You help her see what is good and what is bad. Come, pick up balls. I teach you *Ayo*," Mrs. Fabiyi said, pushing the game across the table and laughing again. "You like frogs, eh, Seth?"

I shrugged and began to pick up the green balls. "They're okay, I guess." Mrs. Fabiyi was right. I did have a responsibility toward Samona. Maybe Samona needed my help.

"Good to eat." Mrs. Fabiyi nodded. "Taste like chicken. I make for you someday."

# CHAPTER

# 10

The one good thing about the beauty contest was that I didn't have to dress up. Manmi rushed us all out of the apartment a whole hour and a half early so we could get good seats. I saw her looking at me funny but she was too busy pushing everyone out the door to bother with me. I had put on Jean-Claude's Yankees baseball cap and some big dark sunglasses that I found in the library at school. I didn't want anybody to recognize me. Last night I had made a decision about Samona. I had to find a way to prove to her that she didn't have to change. I'd done what Papi had said and tried hard to think of life without Samona. It *was* peaceful, just like I'd told Papi. But it was also boring. Then I thought about life with the new Samona in it, and it was just as boring. When I'd tried to help Jean-Claude that Sunday I'd helped to make things better with my family. Now it was time to make things better with Samona.

When we got to the auditorium, Manmi and Granmè made us walk all the way up front and take some seats in the third row. Jean-Claude slouched down in his seat and started snoring right away. I could tell he was faking it. While Papi read the newspaper, Manmi, Granmè and Chantal started talking in whispers about Samona's chances for winning. They kept looking around them like they expected enemy spies to be listening to what they had to say. Then they started talking about what everyone was wearing. Finally, Jean-Claude opened up one eye and said something about beauty contests being about exploitation and that Chantal, Manmi and Granmè were a bunch of "un-feminists." That got Chantal all mad and she leaned toward him and started arguing that beauty contests were getting better and how they weren't all about looks anymore and how about Miss America 1990 who was black and Haitian and smart and in law school but not all that beautiful and that's when I stopped listening. At least they weren't fighting about Jerome anymore. In fact, when Jean-Claude and Chantal did fight now, it was more like the way Samona's brothers and sister fight. It wasn't about serious stuff and they forgot about it almost right away. Most of the time they even seemed to get along.

I got up to look around the auditorium. It was half-full. A lot of people were dressed up in suits and church dresses. You could tell who the parents of the contestants were 'cause they were set up on one side of the stage in the reserved seats. They were looking around all nervous and giving each other fake smiles.

Way in the back I saw Mrs. Whitmore sitting in a seat with a big pole in front of it. I guessed that she didn't have much faith in this new Samona and was expecting the real Samona to make an appearance and embarrass the entire fifth-grade class of Atticus Elementary School.

Way up front, sitting by herself in a white dress with her hands folded in her lap, was Mrs. Roberta Armstrong, Bessie's mother. She was looking straight at the stage and not paying any attention to anyone else around her.

I saw Mrs. Fabiyi marching down the aisle heading for the reserved seating. She had on one of her Nigerian dresses but this one was a whole lot fancier. She had on a new head wrap too that was blue and black and stiff-looking. She looked like an old African queen and everybody turned their heads to stare at her.

Then I saw everyone looking toward the back and I turned to see Samona's family walking in. I could hardly believe it, but Nigel and Anthony were wearing suits and ties. Leticia was in a long dress and there was Mrs. Gemini in a gold lamé miniskirt and a white sequin shirt. She wore long curly hair and spike heels. I knew right away that Mrs. Gemini must be working on one of her stories for the *Intruder* 'cause she keeps her hair in braids all the time and the only shoes she ever wears are black boots. She was holding on to the arm of a short, skinny, lemon-yellow man with round glasses and a red bow tie.

"Hey, y'all," I said, impressed.

"Seth, honey." Mrs. Gemini rubbed my head like she always does and pulled the man up closer to me. "This here is Mistah Biggs."

"Hi, Mrs. Gemini. Mr. Biggs," I mumbled. Now, I knew something was up. Mrs. Gemini never calls me Seth.

*"Asailum malekum,* little brother." Mr. Biggs shook my hand up and down.

"Mr. Biggs is in the Nation of Islam," Mrs. Gemini said in a hushed tone. I saw Leticia, Nigel and Anthony rolling their eyes behind her back.

"Like Malcolm X?" I said, 'cause that was the only thing I could remember about the Nation of Islam.

"Just like Malcolm X," Anthony said with a nod, then mouthed, "kicked out."

"Why don't we all take a seat," Mr. Biggs said, coughing a little.

"Yeah." Leticia smiled, letting Mr. Biggs and her mama lead the way.

"Okay, what's going on?" I asked her quickly.

"Samona ain't told you yet?" Leticia grinned even wider, showing the gap in her front teeth. "Mama's thinking about converting. At least that's what Mr. Biggs thinks. You got to hear this one, Seth."

I watched Leticia, Nigel and Anthony move to the reserved seats, trying not to laugh at Mrs. Gemini's disguise. The old Samona would have told me all about what's going on by now. Mrs. Gemini must be doing that religious assignment she was talking about the last time I'd gone to their house. Just as I sat down in my seat, the lights went off.

A tall, skinny lady with hair piled up on top of her head came out and started speaking into the microphone in the middle of the stage.

"Good evening, ladies and gentlemen, and welcome to the fifteenth annual Little Miss Dorchester contest." The skinny lady was smiling hard enough to make her face crack. She started going on and on about the history of the contest and then she began to introduce the contestants. One by one, fifty-five girls came up and spoke into the microphone.

At first I couldn't tell one from the other. All of them had on frilly yellow, white or pink dresses. Everybody's hair looked fresh from the hot comb. And they all said the same thing.

"Good morning, my name is Aneisha Maron and I live in Dorchester."

"Good morning, my name is Shelita Gordon and I live in Dorchester."

"Good morning, my name is Anita Kayne and I live in Dorchester."

I was thinking they could have left out the "Dorchester" part, seeing as this was the Little Miss Dorchester contest, when Bessie Armstrong came out. She had on a frilly white dress too and her hair was twisted into a bunch of Shirley Temple curls. When she came up to the microphone, I saw her looking at

**109**

her mother. Mrs. Armstrong leaned forward and mouthed the words along with her.

"Hello, ladies and gentlemen, proud members of our community. My name is Bessie Armstrong and I'm proud to call Dorchester my home," Bessie said in a loud voice. She was smiling more than I'd ever seen Bessie smile.

"She's pretty," I heard somebody behind me whispering.

Then, way in the back of the girl who was speaking now, I saw Samona coming across the stage. Only something was different. It wasn't the new Samona. And it wasn't the old Samona. This girl had on a white dress but it wasn't frilly and she had a bright orange and green kente-cloth strip draped across her shoulders. This Samona had her hair in a fancy circle cornrow with bright white beads in it. I knew right away that Mrs. Fabiyi had done it for her. She wasn't wearing a ton of makeup like all the other girls and she wasn't smiling like crazy either. In fact, this girl looked scared.

When it was her turn, Samona walked up to the microphone and whispered, "*Akaroo,* my brothers and sisters. That means 'good morning' in Yoruba. I'm Samona Gemini and I live where you all live: Dorchester."

Then her face split into a big grin and she walked to her place with the rest of the girls. I saw Bessie smiling at Samona. The audience just about went crazy clapping for Samona and I heard people whispering how cute she was. For the first time, I thought—*Could Samona really win this contest?*

The talent segment of the beauty contest started right after that. I've never seen so many girls twirl batons or play the piano before. One even played the tuba. A couple of girls did some tap-dancing. And a whole lot of them sang. The audience clapped the loudest for this one girl, Chiquita Arnold, who just stood there and made faces. Her face must have been made of rubber 'cause she could pull it and stretch it into all sorts of funny and scary faces. Then Bessie came onstage in a pink tutu and did some ballet dancing while twirling *two* batons. She never dropped them once either. Even I was impressed with that.

Finally, Samona came out and she had changed into some old raggedy long skirt and a shirt with holes in the arms. She had a handkerchief wrapped around her head and was carrying a big basket on one arm. I thought, Oh, no. Here it comes! Now Samona would make a fool of herself. But nothing happened. She just stood there, not moving, and staring at the stage. After a long minute, the audience started whispering. Samona looked more scared then she had during her introduction.

Come on, Samona, I said to myself, leaning forward. I was waiting for her pride to kick in. She'd led the way up those stairs to Mrs. Fabiyi's apartment even though I knew she was just as scared as I was. Any minute now

**111**

she would get that hard look in her eyes and then it would be, "Watch out!"

"Come on, Samona," I whispered out loud this time. But Samona didn't do anything and a couple of kids in the audience started calling out, "Get off the stage!"

It was like she was trapped up there. Samona couldn't do anything because she was trying to be somebody normal. Only this somebody normal didn't have Samona's guts or her attitude.

Before I could think about it, I'd jumped out of my chair and into the aisle. Maybe if I yelled at her and called her a bo-bo head she'd snap back to herself. I wasn't sure what I was going to do until I got to the first row and saw Samona still frozen on the stage. She didn't even know I was there. Some people in the audience *were* looking at me so I did the first thing that came into my head.

I flapped my arms.

Then I wobbled my legs and stuck my head out back and forth.

I was doing Samona's funky chicken dance and people in the audience were starting to point at me.

I wobbled down the aisle, flapping harder. I could hear some giggling coming from behind me.

"Oooohhh yeeeaaah!" I sang loudly, like I'd seen Samona do, and then I started shaking my legs in the air one at a time. By now the whole audience was laughing and watching me. I didn't mind. It felt good to just jump around and just act any way I wanted to.

This was what Samona must feel like all the time, I thought.

"Stop that!"

The skinny lady from the stage was coming down the aisle after me, and she was mad. I started wobbling faster, until I was running around the auditorium with the skinny lady chasing after me. I passed Mrs. Whitmore once and saw that she was laughing as hard as the rest of the audience.

When I came back around to the stage, I saw that Samona was laughing too. She had her hand over her mouth to hide it but I could tell. She didn't look scared anymore. I ran back to my seat, where Papi, Manmi, Jean-Claude, Granmè and Chantal were staring at me like they didn't know me. The skinny lady didn't know where I'd sat down. She walked up and down the aisle for a few minutes muttering things like "pageant integrity" before huffing back to the stage.

After everyone quieted down, Samona looked straight into the audience without smiling again and started talking in a loud, serious voice that sounded like an old woman.

> Dat man ober dar say dat woman needs to be lifted ober ditches and to have de best place every whar. Nobody eber helped me into carriages, or ober mud puddles, or gives me any best place—and ar'n't I a woman? Look at me! Look at my arm! I have plowed, and planted,

**113**

and gathered into barns, and no man could head me—and ar'n't I a woman? I could work as much and eat as much as a man (when I could get it), and bear de lash as well—and ar'n't I a woman? I have borne thirteen chilern and seen em mos' all sold off into slavery, and when I cried out with a mother's grief, none but Jesus heard—and ar'n't I a woman?

Samona was doing that speech by Sojourner Truth that Mrs. Whitmore had read to us one day in history class. Samona made every word ring out and put so much feeling into the speech that I forgot she wasn't Sojourner Truth for a while. So did the audience, 'cause Samona got a standing ovation. Manmi had tears in her eyes and Jean-Claude was whistling and clapping his hands off. That's when I started thinking that Samona *deserved* to win the contest. So I wasn't so surprised when after giving the audience a lecture on proper pageant etiquette, the skinny lady announced that Samona, Bessie, Chiquita Arnold and some other girl had made it to the finals.

The next part of the contest was personality and it was pretty boring. The skinny lady just listed the achievements and community work or whatever else the contestants had done that made them look good. While she was doing this, the four finalists came out dressed in new fancy dresses. Then all of them stood in a row and waited for the skinny lady to stop talking and begin the question part of the program. Bessie still looked scared. Samona just looked quiet and serious and the other two girls were smiling their heads off.

Finally, the skinny lady stopped talking about this girl who visited old ladies every Saturday and that girl who tutored after school and announced that the questions would begin. She went up to each girl and asked three questions of each one. The first two were the same of everybody:

"What would you most like to change about our society?"

"If you were on a desert island, what book would you most want with you and why?"

And all the girls gave the same kind of stupid answers. You could tell they must have spent weeks watching recordings of the old Miss America pageants. Everybody was talking about world hunger and AIDS and even American patriotism. She asked one girl about welfare and she said she didn't know anything about welfare 'cause her family supported themselves and she figured everybody should do that and get off welfare. Most of the audience booed her.

Chiquita Arnold said the one thing she wanted to change about the world was school, which everybody laughed at but I thought was the most honest answer. Everybody was making up all that other stuff just so they could look good. Bessie Armstrong said that she wished everybody would be nice to one another. Even

Samona made some stuff up about bringing along Lorraine Hansberry's *A Raisin in the Sun* to a desert island 'cause she thought it was "moving" and "inspiring." I knew Samona's never even read that play. We saw it on TV one Sunday at Samona's house with her aunt Mary, who is crazy about Sidney Poitier movies. That's who Samona's aunt Mary would want on a desert island with her. The real Samona would have asked if she could have an air conditioner or a pool or something more practical than a book.

After the questions, the skinny lady said there would be an intermission while the judges tabulated the votes. Then she said they'd be selling Kool-Aid and cookies right outside the door and everybody started jumping out their seats and rushing up the aisle.

I decided to get up and say hi to Mrs. Fabiyi. She was sitting dead center in the front row and watching the stage like the pageant was still going on. I sat down beside her quietly.

"So, Seth," Mrs. Fabiyi said, still not looking away from the stage. "Samona do good job, eh-eh?"

"Yeah," I said, leaning back against the chairs. "She had the whole thing planned and everybody fooled."

"It good surprise," Mrs. Fabiyi said with a nod, "no?"

"Yeah, I guess." I nodded. "You helped her with all that stuff, didn't you? The speech and the hair? Why didn't she tell me?"

"I help with outside." Mrs. Fabiyi turned her head

away from the stage and stared at me with her old black eyes. "You help with inside. You and Samona good friends."

I swallowed. A good friend wouldn't try and change someone.

"Samona want surprise everyone. You not believe unless you see. No?" said Mrs. Fabiyi.

"No," I admitted. I didn't know Samona could act so well. Maybe I would be nice and go congratulate her after the contest.

"You go with me—behind, after the contest over," Mrs. Fabiyi said, as if she could read my mind.

"Okay." I stood up as the lights started to go down again.

By the time I got back to my seat, the skinny lady was talking again. This time she was saying all this stuff about how every little girl who entered the contest was a winner and how she wished she had fifty-five crowns to give away. The audience started to boo and she shut up and started announcing the winners in a high, excited voice.

"Honorable mention—Miss Bessie Armstrong," she screamed into the microphone.

Everybody started clapping, then Bessie came up to the front of the stage and got a bunch of flowers and a certificate. Her lips were shaking as if she was about to cry. I looked around and saw Mrs. Armstrong leave her seat to rush backstage. I felt real sorry for Bessie.

The skinny lady pulled Bessie over to one corner and made her stand there. Then she read off the next name.

"Second runner-up—Chiquita Arnold," she said, screaming again. This time everybody covered their ears from the screeching of the microphone.

Chiquita walked up to the front of the stage with a big grin on her face. She took the flowers and the certificate and waved to the audience like she had come in first place or something. Then she took her place next to Bessie and started pulling her face into one of those scary faces like she did in the talent segment.

"First runner-up—Samona Gemini," the skinny lady said in a lower voice.

"First runner-up!" Leticia jumped up out of her seat. Then the whole audience was booing and talking. No one could believe Samona hadn't won first place. I heard Granmè shouting in Kreyol that they needed to count the votes again. Nigel and Anthony were saying that it was fixed.

But Samona just walked up to the front of the stage and grinned at all the noise everyone was making. She took her flowers and her certificate and went over and started talking to Bessie Armstrong. Whatever she said must have worked 'cause Bessie stopped crying and started giggling and the two of them hugged each other.

Practically no one heard the skinny lady announce

the winner. Her name was Rosalie Aubry. The skinny lady had all but lost her voice and could barely say her name. And the audience was still talking about fixes and bribes and how Rosalie looked like the judge with the purple dress.

Mrs. Fabiyi came over to get me to go backstage with her and then my whole family and Samona's whole family all decided to go backstage too so there were a bunch of us waiting when Samona came off the stage.

Everybody started hugging and kissing her and telling her that it was a shame she didn't win and how pretty she looked. Samona was smiling and laughing and talking.

Mrs. Gemini kissed Samona on both cheeks. "You conducted yourself like a sunflower."

"Like queen," Mrs. Fabiyi pitched in.

"Like a Nubian princess," Jean-Claude said, tapping her on the shoulder.

Then Samona's family said they were gonna celebrate by going out to the Charthouse, which was a fancy restaurant, and that everybody should come.

In the middle of it all, I got two seconds to talk to Samona.

"I wanted to say congratulations and you should have won," I said real fast. Then I looked her dead in the eye. "Guess you're not *completely* crazy, Samona Gemini."

Samona's eyes were shining straight back into mine. She looked like she was getting ready to say something but Mrs. Whitmore suddenly broke through the crowd and swallowed up Samona in a hug.

"There she is! My star student!" Mrs. Whitmore yelled, squeezing the life out of Samona until Nigel rescued her. Mrs. Whitmore started pulling on Samona's arm and asking her a question and I figured Samona had forgotten all about what I said. Then, right before answering Mrs. Whitmore, Samona turned to look at me and stuck out her tongue.

That's when I knew for sure the old Samona was still there.

## ABOUT THE AUTHOR

JOANNE HYPPOLITE was born in Haiti in 1969. Her family settled in the United States when she was four years old, and she grew up in Boston. She graduated from the University of Pennsylvania with a degree in creative writing and received her master's degree from the Department of Afro-American Studies at the University of California, Los Angeles. She currently lives in Florida, where she plans to pursue her goals of writing and teaching.

*Seth and Samona*, her first novel, won the Second Annual Marguerite de Angeli Prize from Delacorte Press.